"Stare at the picture, Chris. Wish with all your might to go back to 1955."

I did. I concentrated on the photograph with everything I had. Funny that I had never noticed it before, but the clock on the mantel behind my parents read eleven o'clock. I focused as hard as I could on it. Then I tried to imagine that it was twelve hours earlier that same day, that it was eleven o'clock in the morning on December the twenty-fourth in the year 1955—only a short time before Mom and Dad ran into each other. I concentrated harder than I've ever concentrated on anything in my life.

I was getting lightheaded. My staring eyes began to blur and burn. Suddenly the picture began spreading out to an immense size and started rushing up toward me. I felt as though I were about to be swallowed by it. I felt myself slipping off the edge of time as I heard Gail call out my name in a frightened voice that sounded very far away.

Then everything went black. . . .

BERNAL C. PAYNE, Jr.

TRAPPED IN TIME

(FORMER TITLE: IT'S ABOUT TIME)

AN ARCHWAY PAPERBACK
Published by POCKET BOOKS • NEW YORK

Originally published as *It's About Time*

An Archway Paperback published by
POCKET BOOKS, a division of Simon & Schuster, Inc.
1230 Avenue of the Americas, New York, N.Y. 10020

Published by arrangement with Macmillan Publishing Company
Library of Congress Catalog Card Number: 83-24910

ISBN: 0-671-54360-1

First Archway Paperback printing April, 1986

10 9 8 7 6 5 4 3

AN ARCHWAY PAPERBACK and colophon are
registered trademarks of Simon & Schuster, Inc.

Printed in the U.S.A.

IL 7+

To my mother and father,
whose door is always open

TRAPPED
IN TIME

CHAPTER ONE

I wouldn't blame you if you didn't believe this story. If you were telling it to me, I know *I* wouldn't buy it. I'd think you were either a very creative liar or, as my Grandpa Gilbert would say, "your roof wasn't nailed down too tight."

But the difference is that I *know* what happened is true. So what you're going to have to do is trust me, okay? Otherwise you may as well put this book back on the shelf and read something else. Because I'm going to tell you about the king of all nightmares. Mine. Only I couldn't wake up from it. I was stuck inside it and all the screaming and kicking in the world wasn't going to get me out.

It's about a mess my sister and I got ourselves into—a royal mess! I mean, imagine that your mom and dad didn't meet each other when they were teenagers because you got in the way. You heard me right. *You!* And imagine that your very existence hung by a thread because you might have prevented your parents from ever getting married and having you as their kid.

I know it sounds crazy. But that's what happened to us, just the same.

*   *   *

1

I guess I should start out by showing you around so you can see how things are now. That way you can compare them to how they look later. Because there are going to be some big changes. You'll see what I mean.

This is my house. It's a huge old three-story thing that reminds me of a tall white ship rising up out of the ground. It even creaks like a ship. There's a flat area on the roof called a widow's walk with a railing going around it, where I can stand and look out over the town.

Let's go up there and check out the view.

There. Now you can see everything. The name of my town is Summerville. In Missouri. Population, about twenty thousand. The town's full of old houses like mine that were built around the turn of the century. If you look up and down Chestnut Street, you can see a lot of other houses just as tall and old as this one.

Over there, a few blocks away, is Lewis Park, where the pond is. People go there in the summer to picnic and in the winter to ice skate. Down the street, where all those stores are, is our downtown. And if you look over there to the right, you can see the steeple of my church, Christ the King, poking up through those pine trees.

I know Summerville doesn't look too summery, now that it's covered with that six-inch snow we got last night. But summer or winter, it's a nice-looking town, I think. It's a good place to grow up if you're the kind of person who doesn't care for big cities.

Yeah, I know. It's freezing out here. What do you say we go back inside and I'll introduce you to my family.

That's my dad, George Davenport, in the den, poking at the logs in the fireplace. It's Sunday, and this is

2

when he usually reads his history books or catches up on grading tests or papers. He teaches American history at the new Summerville Junior College. Sunday afternoons, during football season, Dad and I sometimes watch the Cardinal games on TV, booing or cheering, depending on which way the game's going. And on Saturday afternoons my mom and dad and sister come to watch our high school team play. That's because I'm on the team. I play wide receiver, first string. But now that football season's over, things are pretty quiet around here on the weekend. So Dad's doing schoolwork today, while I find my own things to do—like tell you this story.

My dad's not bad looking for forty-six. I mean, you have to admit he's still holding up pretty well. Although I did have to get him a new belt for Christmas, because he's suffering from what he calls an "anatomical readjustment." In other words, middle-age spread. Mom even had to let out the waist of his pants another inch. But I don't see much change. Well, not too much.

That's my mom, Elizabeth Davenport—Liz, for short—in the kitchen putting the traditional Sunday roast in the oven. She's a year younger than my dad. She wasn't too wild about turning forty-five, but with her looks, why should she care?

I know. She always heaves those loud sighs when she's in the kitchen. She hates to cook, and she wants us all to hear how much she's suffering. She's not a bad cook, but she isn't a great one, either. She just doesn't put her heart into it. Not the same way she puts her heart into playing the piano. She can do that for hours and never get tired.

Another thing she puts her heart into is her record store in town. After she got her degree in music, and

3

after my sister and I entered kindergarten, she started teaching music at our high school. I guess she taught there ten years. Then she had some kind of argument with the principal and quit to start her own business: the Clarion Music Shop. That was two years ago, and she's been on top of the world ever since. She does grumble a lot about business matters, like taxes and inflation and profit and all that. But underneath it all she's pretty proud of herself, and that's what counts.

That's my sister, Gail, at the kitchen table, typing a paper for school. She's fifteen. She has terrible hand-writing, but she loves to type, so she impresses her teachers by handing in all her reports in neatly typed pages. She's also a straight-A student like our mother was, and she has the same serious, self-conscious face. She's tall like Mom, but, unlike her, Gail's a little on the chunky side down below because she junks it up a lot. She has Mom's reddish brown hair and green eyes and full mouth, but was spared Mom's slightly off-center nose.

So now that you've met everyone, I guess I can get on with my story.

Oh, yeah. I forgot to introduce myself, didn't I? My name's Chris Davenport. I'm sixteen. Seventeen in April.

I look something like my dad. I'm six feet tall and weigh 171 pounds. I inherited Dad's blond hair and blue eyes and straight teeth (thank God I didn't have to wear braces like Gail did). And I have his deep voice—and the Adam's apple that goes with it.

I like to read science fiction, play chess, watch hor-ror movies, play video games, drive my dad's car (when he lets me), go out on dates and, of course, play football—not necessarily in that order.

I also like to write. Someday I hope to write the

Great American Novel. But for now I'm going to practice by telling you this story.

It all started two months ago, on Saturday, December twenty-fourth.

My family has this tradition of not putting up the Christmas tree until Christmas Eve. The custom started with Grandma and Grandpa Davenport, back when Dad was a little boy, and he's kept it alive ever since.

That morning Mom sent Gail and me up to the third-floor attic to bring down our stored Christmas tree ornaments, while Dad and Dr. Bennett—an old family friend—went out to chop down a pine tree on Dr. Bennett's land. At the same time, Mom took off for Bugler's Market to get some last-minute things.

As you can see, our attic is a mess. It's filled with fifteen years of accumulated junk. There's a lot of stuff up here that belonged to my dad's parents, who both died in a car accident when I was a baby. Dad brought most of their trunks and things over from his old house on Elm Avenue and stored it here. He used to say he was going to get around to throwing out some of these things, but I don't expect he ever will. After all, there are a lot of memories in them.

Look at this. Bet you've never seen one of these before. It's Grandpa Davenport's Brownie camera. You look down the viewfinder and see everything upside down. This old camera took some pretty important pictures, as you will see.

Over here are my grandma Davenport's cards: Christmas cards, birthday cards, get-well, and Valentine cards. Hundreds of them. She must have saved every one she ever got, by the looks of it.

And check this out. My grandfather's old railroad

watch. It belonged to his father. The date on it reads 1892. My dad said it probably cost three or four dollars when it was new. It's worth a lot more these days, but he wouldn't take anything for it now.

It's a funny thing. Dad keeps his parents' stuff up here, but I don't think he ever comes up to look at it any more. At least Gail and I have never seen him up here. And it seems like everything is in the same old place, year after year. Probably it'll all be here when my sister and I inherit the house. And if it is, we'll keep it. Especially after what happened in this story. Gail and I want to hang onto Grandma and Grandpa Davenport's things because it would be like always having a part of them with us.

The thing I really wanted to show you is this. It's one of my mom's diaries. She started it back in 1955, when she was sixteen. She'd throw a fit if she knew Gail and I'd been reading it, but to tell you the truth, I think she's forgotten all about it. It's been up here in Grandpa's old desk for as long as I can remember, and it hasn't moved from the drawer in all these years.

And see this? It's a box of old photographs. There are hundreds of them here. Gail and I have spent quite a few dull rainy days up here going through them. This one's a picture of my grandparents taken about a year before their car accident. They're a nice-looking couple, aren't they? Here's another one of Grandpa standing in front of his 1953 De Soto. And here's one I look at every time I come up here. It's a snapshot of my dad and his family with Father Dooley, the priest who used to be the pastor of our church. The back of the picture says: Thanksgiving, 1950.

Ah, here they are. The pictures of my mom and dad I wanted you to see. This one's of them not long after they started going steady, when Mom was sixteen and

Dad was seventeen. They sure have changed, haven't they?

Here's another old picture of Dad, taken the same year, just before he started going with Mom. Would you check out that car he's sitting in! It's a 1930 Plymouth roadster converted into a genuine, sure-thing hot rod. Isn't that unbelievable? To think that my dad owned a hot rod when he was a kid. Look at it. You can't tell from this black-and-white picture, but it was fire-engine red. Fenders and hood stripped off. Engine sticking out. The whole thing lowered to two inches off the ground. And look at those wide white-wall tires and that raccoon tail hanging from the antenna. It even had a real rumble seat.

Dad had a part-time job at a gas station then and did most of the work on the car himself. To him, that car represented power. Not just the kind that's under the hood, with that hopped-up Ford V-8 engine, but a special kind of power that makes a big-league reputation for you. Because when Dad went down the street in his car, people turned their heads. And for him, that had to be the greatest feeling in the world.

Here's another picture of my parents when they were about our age. Every time Gail and I looked at these pictures, we wondered what our mom and dad were like when they were teenagers. It's impossible to look at your parents today and know what they were like when they were young. That was too many years ago. They were different people then. I mean, look at my dad in this snapshot with his hot rod. Now run downstairs and look at him smoking his pipe while grading tests from his American history classes. Can you believe those two are the same person!

You can see in the picture that my dad's hair didn't look anything like it does now. He wears it combed

7

forward now to hide where it's getting thin, but back then it was long and thick and wavy, with long sideburns that were the style in the fifties. There are some similarities in the faces, but notice how *different* he looked then. I don't mean just because he was younger. There's something else, something in his eyes. If you went into the den now and looked at him you'd see that he has that look of—I don't know—I guess, confidence. Like he knows where he's been and where he's going. But in this picture he looks kind of—it's hard to put into words. I guess unsettled is as good as any. Or uncertain. This really made me curious about Dad as a teenager.

Anyway, the more we looked at the old pictures of our parents and read Mom's diary, the more my sister and I wished we could have known our parents when they were our age.

Which takes me back to Christmas Eve, when Gail and I were up in the attic getting the tree ornaments.

──────CHAPTER TWO──────

Like I said before, the house was empty when Gail
and I were up in the attic. And since there was no
need to rush, instead of going straight for the Christmas ornaments, we took a short detour through my
grandpa Davenport's old roll-top desk.

Or what we thought would be a short detour.

There was a snapshot Gail wanted to look at again.
It was of our parents when they first met on Christmas Eve in 1955—twenty-eight years ago. They were
in Dad's living room, standing in front of the Christmas tree, grinning at the camera. Each was holding a
plastic icicle up to the tree, pretending to hang the ornaments on a branch. Gail then flipped to the page in
the diary that went with the picture. "Here it is," she
said, as she sat down on an ancient wooden chest.
Then she read out loud what our mother had written
long ago:

*December 24. I can't believe it! I bumped into
George Davenport after lunch while shopping at
Bradburn's today. I dropped a package and he
picked it up for me and we started talking. Then
he bought me a Coke at Barken's drugstore and
we talked some more. And you know what? He's
not such a bad guy after all. I always thought he*

*was such a show-off, cruising around in his hot
rod, acting like Mister Cool. Personally, I thought
he looked fruit. And his car looks like a red juke-
box. But after talking to him away from all his
flaky friends—especially those cute little chicka-
dees who are always fluttering around him—I realized he's actually a nice guy. He even invited
me to help him get a Christmas tree this afternoon. And tonight he wants me to help him decorate it. Wow!*

Gail rolled her eyes up and sighed theatrically. "Oh,
wow, daddyo." Then she giggled, and I laughed, too.
But our parents' meeting was also something we were
serious about—and very curious.

Gail's eyes dropped for a second, then went back
to the photograph in her hand. "I wonder how Mom
and Dad hit it off when they first met. I mean, what
did they say to each other? How did they feel about
each other?"

"How should I know? Why don't you ask them?"

"I couldn't do that. There are *some* things you just
don't ask about. They're . . . too personal." She slid
her big green eyes over in my direction. "Would you
ask them?"

"Me? Are you kidding? You're the one who wants
to know. You ask."

"Don't give me that baloney, Chris. You'd like to
know about it just as much as I would."

She was right, of course. I did want to know how it
was for Mom and Dad when they met. Did they feel
something for each other right from the start? You
know, the old love-at-first-sight bit. And how did Dad
handle himself when he first talked to Mom? I always
seem to say some idiot thing when I try to impress a

girl, and I wondered if my dad made the same mistakes, too.

Gail read on in Mom's diary.

Christmas morning. Had a great time at George's house last night. The more I know him, the more I take back everything I ever said about him.

Gail halted after that last sentence. "What could Mom possibly have said about Dad? I mean, I know she thought he was a show-off, but did she go around saying bad things about him?"

"Ask her," I suggested.

"Oh, sure. *Hey, Mom, did you think Dad was weird or something before you started going with him?* I mean, really. Come on."

Gail turned to the next page and continued.

All of us—George, his parents, and his sister, Alice—stayed up past midnight decorating the tree, singing Christmas carols, and drinking eggnog. He has a neat family, and I noticed how different he acts when he's around them. He's really a terrific guy. Then George took me home in his circus wagon of a car (I wish he'd get rid of that stupid thing). He shook my hand at the door. I know he wanted to kiss me good night. (What would I have done if he had tried!) He invited me to go skating tomorrow. Double wow!

Gail closed the diary. She had a far-off look in her eyes. "Chris?"

"What?"

"Do you think Mom and Dad were meant for each other? I mean . . . were they destined to fall in love?

11

They're so much alike, I can't imagine them being married to anyone else. Can you?"

"Well," I replied, sitting down in Grandpa Davenport's old rocker, taking the old picture of our parents out of Gail's hand. "No. I can't. Maybe you're right. Maybe they were sort of destined for each other, now that you put it that way."

There was a pause between us. Then Gail uttered those fateful words. "If we could only go back in time to when Mom met Dad. Just to be there to see what it was like."

"Why?" I asked, not really needing to ask.

"You know. Because I'd like to see what it was like for them to come together. It was such a big moment in their lives. And it all happened because Dad bumped into Mom while shopping. Such a small, insignificant thing. And look what the result was. Mom and Dad fell in love, got married, and then us."

"And us, what?"

"Us. You and I are the result of it, too. If it hadn't been for Mom and Dad shopping on that day—if they hadn't bumped into each other at that exact moment—then you and I wouldn't be here talking right now. We would never have been born."

I had to smile at that. "Boy, if you aren't full of profound thoughts today. But you're right. We wouldn't even exist, would we?"

Gail added, "And all because two kids bumped into each other at Bradburn's department store on Christmas Eve in 1955."

Our eyes automatically went to the photograph I was holding. "Wouldn't it be something," I said, "going back to when they met. To actually see it happen."

Gail sighed. "I'd give anything to see that moment. Anything!"

And then I said slowly, remembering something, "You know what? I know this sounds crazy, but . . ."

"But what?"

"Oh, never mind."

"Never mind, what? Come on. Out with it."

"Well, it's just that I read something not too long ago about this psychic woman in some country in eastern Europe who claims she can visit her dead husband—can go back into the past when he was alive—just by looking at an old picture of him." I shrugged. "I know. It sounds screwy. Forget I mentioned it."

Gail gave me one of her skeptical smirks. "You want to run that by me again?"

"Well," I insisted lamely, "that's what the article said. She stares at a picture of her dead husband. She concentrates and puts herself into some kind of trance, and projects herself into the past."

"Projects herself? I don't get it."

"I don't know. I guess she uses her mind to put herself into some kind of time-space warp or something."

"Oh, come on, Chris. You don't really expect me to buy that, do you? This is some more weirdo stuff from out of your science fiction books, right?"

"No. As a matter of fact, I read it in *World Science* magazine when I was doing a paper for my psychology class. I can only tell you what I read. She claims she can concentrate on a certain day and year and go back to that time."

"And when she goes back she walks up to her husband and he sees his wife as an older woman. I bet *that* freaks him out.''

"No. She only sees him from a distance. She doesn't let her husband see *her*."

"What good would that do?"

"I guess she thinks it's better than not seeing him at all."

"And I suppose she sees her other self when she was younger?"

"Yeah. That part was weird, all right. She said it's really hard seeing herself when she's so young and healthy, and there she is all old and wrinkled. She said she likes to go back to the 1920s when she and her husband were just married. She follows the two of them around. Like one time she followed them when they went for a walk in a park, and another time she sat behind them at an outdoor concert."

"That's ridiculous," Gail objected. "How in the world can an old version of yourself be with a young version? There can't be two of you around at the same time, can there? Anyway, how can anyone go back in time just by looking at a picture? People all over the world would be flying back into the past all the time."

"Not really," I replied, warming to the subject. "This woman claims that probably one person in a hundred million can do it. The thing is, these few people don't even know they have the power to project themselves into the past, because they never tried to do it."

Gail's expression softened, but she still looked skeptical.

"All I know is, she stares at certain pictures of her and her husband and forces herself out of the present into the past. Like a superwish. If she wants to see her husband in 1925, for instance, she finds a picture that was taken back then, stares at it, and wishes herself back to that time."

Gail pursed her lips like she always does when she's deep in thought. She looked down at the diary, then took the picture of our parents out of my hand and studied it for a long moment. When she spoke, her voice sounded far away.

"Wouldn't . . . that . . . be . . . something?" Her head suddenly shot up. She was wide-eyed with excitement. "Chris, I know this sounds crazy, but—why don't we give it a try?"

"What? Oh, come on, Gail. Maybe I read all that stuff, but that doesn't mean I believe it."

She looked at me hopefully, like she does whenever she wants me to do something for her—the kind of look that tugs at you and won't let go. "Come on, Chris. Won't you even try? For me?"

"It's totally asinine. I'm sorry I even mentioned it." I gave her a sidelong glance. "You're not really serious, are you?"

Wearing her most genuine earnest expression, Gail leaned toward me, her eyes riveted to mine. "Admit it, Chris. You'd like to go back to when Mom and Dad met. To actually *be* there."

"Sure, but—"

"How do we know we can't do it? Maybe we're among the few who *can* go back into the past."

"Well—"

"We have the right kind of picture," she insisted, holding the photograph up to me. "It was taken on the day they ran into each other at the store. The day that started their whole lives together."

"You *are* serious!"

"Wouldn't you give anything to see Mom and Dad meet that day?"

15

"Yeah, but—"

"Okay, then. Let's try. It can't hurt, can it? Sit over here," she ordered. "Come on."

Reluctantly, I got up and sat beside her, just to humor her. What did I have to lose, anyway? No one was around to see how idiotic we were acting. And Gail wouldn't tell anyone about it. So what the heck, I thought. I'd try it for a minute, and then we'd get back to doing what we were doing.

"Now, then," she began determinedly. "We'll stare at this picture of Mom and Dad and—"

"And what? Teleport ourselves back to 1955? Shouldn't we pack a suitcase or something? At least take a toothbrush with us?"

"Come on, Chris. Just stare at the picture with me." She poked me in the ribs medium hard. "Come on!"

So I did what she wanted, a little surprised that she was carrying this thing so far.

Now then, I have to admit that at that moment I felt a growing excitement. One side of me said that the whole thing was totally dumb, but the other side felt like Gail did. What if such a power did exist? What if we *were* among the few people on earth who could wish themselves back in time?

Gail held the picture of our parents between us. Her voice sounded strange as she began chanting in a low, serious voice: "Stare at the picture, Chris. Stare at Mom and Dad as hard as you can. Wish with all your might to go back into the past. Back to when the picture was taken. Back to Christmas Eve, 1955. December twenty-fourth, 1955. Stare at them . . . stare . . . wish . . . wish as hard as you can . . . harder . . . harder . . . harder. . . ."

I did. I concentrated on the photograph with everything I had. There they were, two kids who would be our future parents, who hadn't the slightest idea that they would someday get married. That they would end up spending the rest of their lives together and have us as their children.

I kept staring at the picture, concentrating on it with every ounce of mental energy I had.

Funny that I had never noticed it before, but the clock on the mantel behind my parents read eleven o'clock. I focused as hard as I could on it. I kept repeating to myself that it was eleven o'clock at night when the picture was taken. Then I tried to imagine that it was twelve hours earlier that same day, that it was eleven o'clock in the morning on December the twenty-fourth in the year 1955—only a short time before they ran into each other at noon at Bradburn's department store. I concentrated on that one image harder than I've ever concentrated on anything in my life.

I was getting lightheaded. My staring eyes began to blur and burn. But I kept all my attention on the picture, wishing, wishing that I could go back to that time so many years ago, back to the single most important moment in my parents' lives. For that matter, the most important moment in *our* lives.

Suddenly the picture of my parents with the tree and ornaments and mantel and clock began spreading out to an immense size and started rushing up toward me. I felt as though I were about to be swallowed by it. I felt myself slipping off the edge of time as I heard Gail call out my name in a frightened voice that sounded very far away.

Then everything went black.

──────CHAPTER THREE──────

I slowly came to, not knowing where I was. I felt dazed, and everything was spinning like a merry-go-round gone insane. I couldn't move. I struggled to lift my head, but the room kept whirling, throwing me back down. And then it began to slow up, until everything around me finally rocked to a gentle rest.

I opened my eyes, trying to focus on the rafters above me. Then I rolled my head over and spotted Gail lying next to me. I opened my mouth, but all I could get out was, "Gaaaailll. . . ."

I heard my sister's weak voice. "Chrissss. . . ."

"Are you . . . all right?"

Gail opened her eyes, blinking at me. "Chris . . . ? What happened? I'm . . . so . . . dizzy."

We both moved an inch, then another and another, until we were able to help each other up to a sitting position. We sat there, waiting for our heads to clear. And when they did, we felt the shock of our lives.

Gail said it first. "Chris! Look! Everything's changed!"

We staggered to our feet, looking around with unbelieving eyes. The attic had changed, all right. There wasn't one thing in it that we could recognize. There were some boxes and suitcases neither of us had ever seen before. Other than that, the place was cold and empty.

We looked at each other, wide-eyed and horrified.

Gail gasped, "Chris! It worked! My God, we did it!"

All I could do was stand there, looking around, shaking my head, trying to digest what was happening.

I took an unsteady step toward the doorway, but Gail was ahead of me. I stumbled down the attic stairs behind her in complete panic, hoping against hope that everything else in the house was unchanged. But I knew it wouldn't be, and it wasn't.

We ran into my bedroom and didn't recognize a thing. The color of the walls and rug was different. The furniture was different. The clothes in the closet were different. We darted over to Gail's room next and found it completely empty, except for some boxes stacked up against one wall. Then we ran to our parents' room. Again, there wasn't anything in it that was familiar. The whole time I kept repeating, "No, no, this can't be, can't be, it's not true, it's a dream. . . ." But, of course, it wasn't a dream.

We flew down the stairs. Everything was changed. It was as though suddenly we had been plunked into someone else's house. Only this was *our* house!

"Chris! Look!" Gail pointed a shaky finger toward a calendar on the kitchen wall.

I walked over to it and felt goose bumps break out all over me. "Oh my God! It's true!" The date on it read: December 1955!

I stood there, weaving a little on my rubbery legs, staring at the date, shaking my head.

"Chris! It worked! We actually went into the past! We're here in 1955! Isn't it great!"

"Yeah," I replied, combing my fingers through my hair, blinking around, trying to maintain my sanity. "Sure. Real great." And the first clear thought that popped into my jumbled head was, "Now that we're in the past, how do we know we'll be able to go back to the future?"

"We'll just wish our way back," my sister replied. "Now we know we can do what the woman in that magazine can do. If she can go into the past and come back, so can we. We're the few people on earth she was talking about. This is fantastic!"

Fantastic was the right word, but not in the sense my sister meant.

Another thought popped into my head. "If this is our house in '55, then where are the people who live here? If they walk in now, we're sunk!"

We both looked through the kitchen to the front door, expecting it to open as the shocked owners walked in. Then our eyes scanned the kitchen, searching for we didn't know what. I was getting panicky. "We better get out of here, Gail. I mean now!"

But she was walking up to the calendar, staring at it. "Wait, Chris. Look at this. Here on the twenty-second. Somebody wrote in: TWA. 124. 9:20."

"That must be it," I said. "Call the airport. Find out where flight 124 went while I look around." I ran upstairs and found the closets and drawers nearly empty. By the time I went back downstairs, Gail was hanging up the phone, wearing a smile.

"Flight 124 went to Miami, Florida. Looks like whoever lives here flew south for Christmas."

"I sure hope it was for Christmas." With that out of the way, another thought occurred to me. "You know what? We're assuming today *is* the twenty-

20

fourth. But what if it's not? The calendar says it's December, 1955. But what day?''

"It has to be the twenty-fourth," Gail insisted, "because that's what we wished for."

"But we don't know that for sure."

Old eagle-eyed Gail spotted a newspaper in the back hall trash can and read the date. "It says December the twentieth!"

"But that still doesn't tell us what *today* is," I complained. "We don't know how old that paper is." I glanced at the front page of the Summerville *Courier* and saw a photograph of President Eisenhower and his wife holding hands with a little girl who was wearing leg braces. The caption of the photo read: IKE REACHES OUT. WHY DON'T YOU?

I must have turned a little pale, because Gail asked, "What's wrong?"

"What's wrong?" I exclaimed. "It's really starting to hit me. This *is* 1955!"

But the shock had already worn off my sister, and she was actually smiling. "Come on, Chris, let's look around. This is really something, isn't it?"

Oh, it was something, all right. You have no idea how strange it was for us to walk through our own house, knowing that it wasn't our house. It wouldn't belong to our parents until 1969, when I was the ripe old age of one.

We explored the first floor, experiencing the uneasy feeling of seeing all sorts of unfamiliar things. The furniture in the living room and dining room was blond Scandinavian instead of the dark mahogany Queen Anne my parents loved so much. The kitchen was painted turquoise, the living room was a hideous pink, and the sunroom was filled with white bamboo furniture that would have made my mother gag. The kitchen cabinets were white enamel instead of wood, and in place of our new bronze stove and refrigerator, we found more plain white.

I opened the freezer and saw that it was caked with ice. Frost-free refrigerators apparently weren't around yet. And naturally there was no microwave, like we had. No one in 1955 had heard of them.

The TV in the living room was a large console but, of course, it was the latest model in black-and-white, since color hadn't come on the market yet. And the wooden Philco record player with the swing-out doors was anything but stereo. The only records I saw inside its cabinet were those ancient heavy 78s that break so easily.

I was dizzy from running around the house, looking at all these changes. I didn't want to see any more. I sat down on a flowered couch in the living room and leaned over, burying my face in my hands.

"Chris?" Gail sat down beside me. "Are you all right?"

"No," I said through my sweating hands. "I don't like this. I want to go back."

"What?"

My head shot up. "I said I want to go back! Now!"

"But why? Are you scared?"

"Darn right, I'm scared! Aren't you?"

"Sure. A little. But so what? Think of us as—as explorers. Don't you see what we've done?"

"The question is, do *you* see what we've done?" I swung around and gestured at all the strange things in our house. "This is serious, Gail! This isn't like traveling to a foreign country or something. At least then we'd know we could get back. But we've traveled in *time*! We might be stuck here for the rest of our lives!''

My sister jumped up with that stubborn expression she sometimes gets. ''All right then, *you* go back. But I'm staying!''

''Gail,'' I began. ''This is—''

''—the greatest thing that has ever happened to us,'' she finished. ''No,'' she said flatly. ''I'm not going to let this slip through my fingers.'' She flung herself back down beside me. ''Oh, Chris, how can you think of going back now that we're here?''

''Because neither of us even knows for sure if we *can* get back! We've got to try. Now!''

She got up again and paced the room angrily. ''Then go! I'm not leaving! I'm going to be there when Mom and Dad meet if it's the last thing I do!''

And I shouted back, ''It just might be the last thing you do!''

Neither of us said anything for a couple of seconds. Then Gail said, ''I can't go back, Chris. Don't you understand? I *need* to see this. We won't be gone that long. Please, Chris.''

My sister knew just where to hit. She knew I wouldn't desert her. ''All right,'' I sighed. ''I'll stay. But not long. And you better hope nothing goes wrong with our going back.''

Just then a grandfather clock in the front hall chimed the quarter hour. Gail spun toward the sound and looked at the time. ''It's almost noon. Mom and Dad met at Bradburn's at noon! If today's the twenty-fourth, we've got to hurry!''

She was almost at the front door when I yelled, ''Hold it!''

Gail halted with her hand on the doorknob. ''Why?''

23

"First of all, if anyone sees us running out of this house—it isn't ours, remember?—they're going to call the police. And, second, I'm not going outside with only a sweater on." I pulled back the closed drapes a crack. "Look out there. It's probably freezing. Now calm down and let's do this thing right. Let's see if we can't find something around here to wear."

We looked in the closets and found some slightly undersized coats that belonged to the present owners of our house. We also picked up some knit gloves and mufflers. We put them on and stared at ourselves in the front hall mirror. Gail looked me over, grinning. "You look like something out of a late night movie."

I had to admit that blue jeans and a long brown top coat, with my arms hanging out, weren't going to put me on the top-ten-best-dressed-men-in-America list. But I had to wear something. "You're looking pretty sharp yourself," I came back.

Gail frowned at her double-breasted, black-and-yellow plaid wool coat. "I look like an old lady! I can't go out looking like this!"

"Sure you can. This is 1955. For all you know, you're right in style."

Gail gave me a smirk. "This rag wasn't in style at *any* time!"

We both headed for the front door. "Hold it," I said. "We can't go out that way. Remember?"

"Then let's sneak out the back way," Gail suggested.

We went to the back of the house and glanced out all the windows to see if anyone was around. It was cold outside and there wasn't a soul in sight. So we unlocked the back door latch and walked down the porch steps just as casually as two thieves, and strolled down the driveway to the front sidewalk. Luck was on our side; no one saw us. We both breathed a sigh of relief. And no sooner had we done that than we started looking around.

"Chris! Look!"

And we gazed at the world of 1955.

————CHAPTER FOUR————

Our first shock on Chestnut Street was the absence of many familiar houses. All we could see were vacant lots. Most houses in our neighborhood simply hadn't been built yet. If that wasn't strange enough, we realized that none of our friends lived here any more, because they hadn't even been born! And, in some cases, we were now older than our friends' parents.

The real mind-blower was the cars we saw as we strolled down our neighborhood streets. They were all so old-fashioned, yet so new looking. Some were huge shiny things loaded down with chrome, with grilles that made bizarre metal faces at you. Some of the names I'd never heard of before, like Packard, Willys, Studebaker, Frazer, Hudson, Nash. But even the cars with familiar names looked pretty strange. Especially the ones that were made in the 1930s and '40s. Most of these oldies but goodies were extinct in 1983. Now they were all around us, looking just as normal as could be.

When we reached downtown, we were stunned by all the transformations. Old buildings were standing where new ones would eventually take their places. Vacant lots stood where bustling stores would later be built. There were plenty of old familiar buildings around that are still standing in our time, but most of them had different names on their windows.

We were passing a store when Gail stopped and stared through the window. "Holy cow!" She pointed to a display of women's clothes. "Would you look at that!"

I did. "So what's the big deal? That's the way women dressed in the fifties."

"No," my sister corrected me. "The prices! Look at them!"

She was right. They were practically giving their clothes away, compared to today's prices. There was a wool dress for forty dollars, a blouse for four, shoes for nine, hats for five.

"I can't believe it!" she exclaimed.

But there was a lot more of that to come.

We walked a little farther and glanced into a restaurant that would later become a video game parlor (where I've lost my share of quarters). The menu on the wall said hamburgers were twenty-five cents, Cokes five cents, French fries fifteen, and malts twenty. Suddenly I understood what the phrase "good old days" meant to my parents.

We passed a gas station that had a big sign out front: GAS WAR. At first I imagined some kind of war with the OPEC countries. But this was 1955, and OPEC hadn't even been formed yet. A gas war in the 1950s meant that one gas station was trying to sell gasoline cheaper than its competitor down the street. And the one I saw was doing a pretty good job of it, because it was selling gas at 22.9 cents per gallon!

"Can you believe it?" I nearly shouted. "A person could fill up for practically nothing! If these people only knew that gas will some day cost a *dollar* and twenty-two cents a gallon."

27

Gail answered, "They'd never believe it. I'm sure they'd say it couldn't happen."

We stopped at the first drugstore we came to, to check the date in the newspapers. The interior looked like it came out of the 1920s. It was all white marble and dark wood, with ceiling fans rotating slowly over a checkerboard floor. Two pinball machines stood off in a corner, and the strong smell of medicine hung in the air.

The first thing we did was head for the newspapers, which were stacked next to the magazine rack. I picked up a *St. Louis Post Dispatch*. It read: Thursday, December 23, 1955.

We had arrived a full day ahead of time!

"How can that be?" Gail asked, as we sat down with the paper at the soda fountain, staring down in disbelief at the date.

I shook my head. "You got me."

"Maybe we did something wrong in the attic," she suggested.

"Well, I think we did a pretty good job, considering we went back twenty-eight years and only missed the mark by one day. Not bad for the first time, I'd say."

A very old soda jerk in a stiff white jacket and paper hat strolled up to us. "What'll it be, kids?"

I pulled out my wallet and saw that I had only three bucks. Not much to go on. Gail dug into her blue jeans, coming up empty. Then she looked at the prices on the wall and kicked my leg under the counter. I followed her eyes and smiled. I'd forgotten. We were semirich by 1955 standards. We ordered hamburgers, French fries, and Cokes, for a total of one dollar for both of us, plus two cents tax.

A new worry came to me as we ate. I said to Gail

in a low voice, "Do you realize what's going on back home? Our real home? I know Dad will be gone for a couple of hours, but Mom should be back by now. She's going to wonder where we disappeared to."

Gail swallowed and looked thoughtfully at the bite she had just taken out of her sandwich. "Didn't Mom say she was going over to look in on Gram? [our grandma Gilbert] You know she does that every time she goes shopping. She usually picks up something for Gram and takes it over, and then they gab for an hour or so."

"Yeah. I guess you're right. Maybe we don't have to rush back yet. But let's not stay too long. We can always try coming back tomorrow. After all, it's tomorrow we wanted in the first place. If we *can* come back again," I added.

"Oh, don't be such a worrywart. If we can do it once—"

"Yeah, I know, we can do it again."

"What time is it?"

I glanced down at my watch. "Almost twelve. We'll look around a bit more and head back. Agreed?"

"Agreed."

We went back outside and looked around town some more, feeling a little like space travelers on an alien planet. We walked over to Mom's music store and weren't all that surprised to see a gift shop there instead.

As any normal, red-blooded American teenagers would do, Gail and I stopped at a record store down the street (no longer around) to see what the people of the fifties were listening to. Knowing that today's rock music was born during the fifties, we looked around for the area marked rock 'n' roll. I guess we had expected the store to dedicate half its space to rock 'n' roll, but all we found was a short stack of records. This kind of music was still in its infancy; it would grow into a giant later.

I thumbed through a stack of 78s and that new invention called the 45. I read the names of old rock 'n' roll stars from days of yore: Bill Haley and the Comets, Little Richard, Fats Domino, Ray Charles, the Drifters, and Chuck Berry.

"School out already?"

Gail and I spun around at the voice of a short, middle-aged man, as he came out from the back room. He was wearing a yellow bow tie, a blue sweater, and a friendly smile.

All I could answer was, "Oh, hi."

"They said they were going to let school out a little early today for Christmas vacation." Then he added, "Don't think I've seen you kids in here before. Have I?"

Gail replied, "No. We're new in town. Just thought we'd stop in and look around a little."

"Go right ahead. I see you're looking at the rock and roll records. I don't stock much of that stuff here. Don't care for that kind of noise myself. It's just a fad that'll blow over. Soon, I hope."

"I don't know," I replied. "It just might stick around."

"Think so?" He rubbed his chin meditatively for a second, eyeing the rock 'n' roll sign. "Then it'll be the end of music as I know it." His smile came back. "Oh, well. It's you kids who buy most of the records now. I guess if that's the kind of music you want, that's what you'll get."

We both smiled and thanked the man. Then Gail and I went back out into the winter air.

"Chris," Gail said, as she buttoned up against the

cold, "let's go up to school and see what it looks like."

From a block away, Summerville High still looked pretty much the same, but as we got closer we began feeling again that eerie sensation of walking back into the past. School was just letting out, and students were beginning to pour out the front doors.

A lot of the girls wore bright red lipstick and nail polish, and quite a few had their hair done up in ponytails. Most of them were wearing long, tight skirts, or pleated ones, with tight sweaters. And I think every girl had on either penny loafers or saddle shoes with white bobbysocks.

Some of the boys had short crew cuts, others had long hair that came together in back in what was called a D.A., and quite a few had huge waves pushed up in front and slicked down with hair cream. Some guys had these baggy slacks that tapered down to the tightest cuffs I've ever seen. The hoods walked around in black leather motorcycle jackets with their collars turned up, trying to look tough. But most of the guys were wearing our school jackets of gold and black, while others had on blue suede jackets. I noticed that a few boys wore pink shirts and dark gray pegged pants with thin white belts. From what I've heard, they were the rage back then.

Nowhere did we see a girl in jeans or a guy in sneakers. Except for the hoods, everyone looked dressed up by 1983 standards. And, even without pulling a surprise bust, I knew that there wasn't a doper in the crowd. Probably most of these kids didn't know the first thing about drugs—the illegal kind, that is. And the chances were that most of them wouldn't even have cared. That problem was to come later.

And the cars! What a sight! Customized cars right out of Dad's ancient issues of *Hot Rod* magazine started parading around the grassy circle in front of school. Cars with ooga horns and bells and wolf whistles; cars with dual aerials and spotlights and dice hanging from mirrors; cars lowered in front or in back or all the way around; cars with all the chrome taken off, including the door handles; and all of them blasting away with dual glasspack mufflers that made deep throaty sounds. Nineteen fifty-one Mercurys, '50 Oldsmobiles, '49 Chevys, and '48 Fords cruised around the front of the school. A few motorcycles and motor scooters roared and backfired. There were even some hot rods with hopped-up engines uncovered and on display. One was a '32 Ford covered with primer that looked like it was in that uncertain stage between junk and the finished product. And there was a bright red hot rod with the top down: a roadster, chopped and channeled, with a rumble seat in back and a huge engine sticking out in front—a V-8 with a huge chrome air cleaner sitting on top of a four-barrel carburetor—that must have guzzled gas like it was, well, like it was only twenty-two cents a gallon.

Because of all the commotion going on around me, it took a few seconds for what I was looking at to register. And when it did, it nearly knocked me over. "Gail!" I whispered loudly, pulling her over to me. "Over there! Look who it is!"

She turned to see where I was looking. It took her a few seconds, too. Then her mouth flew open like mine had. "Dad!"

Yes, dear reader, there he was, sitting behind the wheel of that fire-engine red roadster of his, wearing an equally bright red satin jacket. It was our father:

32

seventeen and trim, with long blond hair blowing in the wind. A kid just a little older than me!

While we stood gawking, a girl dashed passed us, yelling and waving at our teenage father. "Sonny! Hey, Sonny!" Her long black hair swung behind her as she ran toward Dad's car.

I whispered to Gail, "That girl called Dad 'Sonny.' Our father was nicknamed Sonny? How come we never knew *that*?"

But Gail was gripping my arm as she watched the ponytailed, saddle-shoed, long-skirted girl jump into "Sonny's" hot rod. My sister gasped. "Did you see who that was that got in Dad's car?"

"Yeah. Pretty good looking, I'd say."

"I don't mean that," she said, squinting at the girl. "Didn't you recognize her? Add twenty-eight years to her age, then you will. That girl was Becky Mc-Connell. My English teacher!"

We stared dumbfounded at our father and Gail's future teacher (whose name was Steel then)—both kids around our age, sitting in a hot rod only a few yards away. I felt my brain starting to go numb on me. Everything was becoming unreal. We knew we were going to see our father as a kid when we came back into the past, but I was still freaking out anyway.

Dad, unaware that his future children were watching him, started gunning his engine. Thunder roared out of the dual tailpipes over and over, blasting the street with noise and blue exhaust.

I was suddenly embarrassed. That was my father over there showing off! Just like a kid!

Then we heard a girl's voice behind us: "Look. There's Sonny Davenport with Becky Steel. I wish I was in *her* place. He's such a dream."

Another girl's voice replied, "Sonny Davenport's a conceited fathead. You can have him."

Gail and I automatically swung around to see who would say such a rotten thing about our father. The girl's eyes were green, her hair reddish brown, and her face was long and narrow. In the style of the times, she wore bright red lipstick and pink rouge. She had on a conservative gray winter coat with matching gloves, and white socks with black loafers. She was slim, tall, and attractive.

My sister and I were on the verge of telling this girl where to get off for calling our dad a fathead, when we both halted in complete astonishment. Because we were staring at our teenage mother!

The girl standing beside our young mother was saying, "You may think Sonny's a fathead, but I know fifty girls who'd go out with him in a second. Including yours truly."

Our girl-mother answered, "Then you and those fifty girls would be going out with the biggest show-off in town. If he didn't have that hot rod, he wouldn't have anything."

I blushed, but not from the cold, as we all heard Dad gunning his engine, attracting everyone's attention.

The other girl cocked her head at Mom. "You know what, Liz? I think you're just a little bit jealous."

"Oh, come on, Vera," Mother said with a forced laugh. "Me, jealous? Of whom? Becky? I wouldn't go out with George Davenport for all the tea in China. He may be good looking, but he probably has feathers for brains. I mean, look at that *thing* he drives."

"Oh, yeah?" Vera retorted. "Well, at least Sonny and *that thing* are exciting and fun to be with."

"What's that supposed to mean?" Mom asked.

"Oh, nothing," Vera replied innocently. "And who are *you* riding home with, Liz? As if I didn't know."

Mom frowned and was about to say something, when a car horn made her turn around toward the crowded street.

"Speaking of the devil," the other girl said, regarding the new white 1955 Oldsmobile 88 that had stopped in front of them. "There's your James Dean, Liz. Driving his mommy's new car."

"Very funny, Vera."

The other girl walked away, calling back, "See ya later, alligator."

"Sure," Mom growled. "In a while, *crocodile*!" Then she hurried out to the street and jumped into the waiting car.

"Chris!" Gail swallowed. "Look at the driver of that car Mom just got into. Don't you see who it is? It's Dr. Bennett!"

My head was really in a tailspin now. Out there in the car-jammed street was my seventeen-year-old father, sitting in a red hot rod with a girl version of Gail's future English teacher. In the car right behind them was our sixteen-year-old mother with a teenage Dr. Bennett, who is not only a friend of the family, but the very doctor who brought Gail and me into the world! But the real mind-blower was that Dr. Bennett and my dad could be two adults out chopping down a Christmas tree in 1983, and at the same time, two kids driving away from a hard day in high school.

I mean, this whole thing was genuinely bonkers!

We heard Dad gun his hot rod, blasting Dr. Bennett's—or should I say eighteen-year-old John Bennett's—car with exhaust fumes and thunder. I could see by Mom's frowning face that she was saying

something about Dad to Bennett. Something not too
kind, by the look of it. Then both cars inched their
way around the grassy circle in front of the school and
disappeared down the street with a small parade of
other jam-packed cars and motorcycles right behind
them.

Gail summed up the whole thing as she watched
Mom and Dad driving away in separate cars, "Oh, no!
This is awful! Mom doesn't like Dad at all! Did you
see them? They're as opposite as can be!"

"Gail," I said, "what are you worried about, anyway? Mom and Dad are happily married to each other.
Remember? What we're seeing is the past. No matter
how it looks now, we know what's going to happen in
the future. So why worry about it?"

Gail didn't look too convinced. "But you heard
what she said about Dad. And didn't you see how she
looked at him just now? They're like complete
strangers!"

"Well," I said, "they obviously know about each
other. But it's going to turn into more than just that
soon. Remember, they're going to run into each other
at Bradburn's tomorrow. Then things will change."

Gail squinted down the street. "Let's follow them
and see what happens."

"Sure, Gail. Real good. We're walking, remember?"

"Then let's at least head down Jefferson after them.
That's where everyone's going. Maybe we'll see
something."

So we did.

CHAPTER FIVE

We walked quickly down Jefferson Avenue for only three blocks, when right across the corner of Lewis Park, we found the after-school hangout everyone had headed for. It was a drive-in called Hamburger Heaven (which has since gone to hamburger heaven and been replaced by the ever-popular McDonald's). I suddenly remembered my dad telling me about the Hamburger Heaven "of the old days"—about how cars used to pile up there after school, and how everyone would run around from car to car talking to one another, while carhops scurried about taking orders and delivering food. Each car radio was tuned to WIL, the station that covered that revolutionary trend in music called rock 'n' roll.

By the time Gail and I got there, the lot was jammed with an assortment of customized cars, convertibles, jalopies, motorcycles, and conservative "daddy's cars." The aroma of burgers and fries and barbecue sauce wafted about in the cold air. Loud, laughing voices filled the parking lot, while Bill Haley and the Comets belted out "Rock Around the Clock" on every car radio.

Gail and I sat at a wooden picnic table on the edge of the lot. Fortunately, the sun was beginning to peek through the clouds, warming things up a little. From

where we sat we could easily watch Dad and Mom.
Dad's hot rod was parked beside John Bennett's white
Olds 88, with Dad's side right next to Mom's.

Even though it was cold out, kids had their windows or tops down, radios blared, cigarettes burned.
Everyone either talked into a neighbor's car or yelled
over cars, making plans for dates, joking, flirting,
shooting straw wrappers, spilling Cokes on window
trays, giving the carhops trouble, and, in general,
having what they called "a ball." Dad's top was down,
of course, and he was doing more than his share of
adding to the noise. But Mom and John Bennett had
their windows up, and were sitting quietly in their car,
sipping Cokes, their lips moving every once in a while.

Gail and I ordered two hot chocolates and tried not
to look like complete idiots, sitting outside in the cold.
We also tried to appear casual as we glanced at our
parents. Not much of anything was happening: Dad
was wolfing down a burger and saying something
funny to his friends, while Mom seemed to be ignor-
ing all the action around her.

All of a sudden, a blast of pipes came roaring down
the street. As a spanking new green 1955 Thunderbird
sports car pulled in, every voice on the lot fell quiet,
and all eyes turned toward the gleaming machine. Two
well-dressed guys got out and headed over to Dad's
car. The guy who had been riding shotgun sneered to
his companion in a loud voice, "Well, look who's
here, Wild Bill. It's Sonny Davenport and his little red
wagon."

"Hey, Sonny," the T-bird driver said to my dad in
a slow, even voice. "How ya doin'?"

The guy was obviously forcing his mouth into a grin,
but it didn't have anyone fooled.

When Dad didn't respond, the T-bird driver said,

"Think you're ready to go against me again, Sonny boy? You took me when I was running automatic, but I just put in four on the floor and my bird's gonna eat you up."

Dad looked over at this Wild Bill character casually, then at the new green sports car, then back at him, and drawled, "Your bird still looks more like a green *chicken* to me, Willy William. Why don't you drag Bennett over there? I've got better things to do." He finished off his Coke with a loud slurp and winked at Becky, who was obviously enjoying all the attention as much as Dad.

It got so quiet you could have heard a French fry drop.

"You callin' me chicken, Sonny boy?" the guy snarled.

"No," Dad answered nonchalantly. "It's just that I don't want any of your green chicken feathers clogging up my new air cleaner when I blow you off the road."

Becky let out a giggle for Wild Bill's benefit.

"Think you're pretty cute, don'tcha, Sonny boy?" Wild Bill squared off.

Gail eyed me as I stood up, ready for action. If either of those two clowns tried anything with my dad, I was going to jump in and help.

Wild Bill's grin stretched wider. "I've got fifty bucks that says my bird poops all over your little red wagon. How's that sound to you, Sonny boy? You on?"

I could see that Dad was uneasy about this. Fifty dollars was a small fortune. This guy was apparently some rich kid with money to burn. But Dad handled the situation like a champ.

"I don't want your money," Dad answered, as more

kids got out of their cars to hear the two combatants. "I've got a better idea. How about if the loser can't use his car for a week? And just to make sure he doesn't, he has to park it in front of the winner's house and leave it there for that week. Sort of like a victory trophy for everyone to see. How does that grab you, Willy William?" Dad chuckled. "I wouldn't mind having your bird roosting in front of my house. Anyway," he added, glancing around at his friends, "my mom could use the eggs." Dad looked over at Becky and gave her a slight nod. She opened her door and got out, smiling.

Eager faces turned toward Wild Bill, as a murmur rippled through the crowd.

"You're on, Sonny boy," Wild Bill snarled through his teeth. "Right now! From here to the graveyard. Let's do it!"

Then all hell broke loose. Horns honked for car-hops to take trays, bills were paid, kids shouted instructions to one another, cars pulled out onto Jefferson with a rumbling of mufflers.

The drag was on.

Cars left the lot as kids drove away to watch the contest. Some stayed in front of Hamburger Heaven, while others drove down Jefferson to the Summerville graveyard gates. Others posted themselves at various points along the way.

Dad's red hot rod and Wild Bill's green Thunderbird had backed out onto the street where they now waited, lined up, engines revving, tailpipes growling, like two snarling dogs straining at their leashes.

My heart was pounding as we watched a tall boy standing in front of the two cars with his hand up. Wild Bill was hunched over his wheel, glaring at Dad, while

Dad sat calmly, looking straight ahead down the street. A car horn down Jefferson gave three long blasts. That must have been the signal that the coast was clear, because the boy dropped his hand and both cars shot forward, tires screeching, engines roaring, gears whining, mufflers machine-gunning all the way down the street, leaving behind a sickening smell of burnt rubber and exhaust. Bystanders yelled as the two cars raced past them, cheering the draggers on. I dashed out into the street to see who was winning, but by that time both cars had disappeared over the rise.

The next thing we heard was cheering in the distance and then the sound of cars coming back. Dad's hot rod led the parade of honking cars returning slowly down the street. One by one, they all pulled back into the parking lot, gave a final victory blast from their mufflers, then shut off their engines. Everyone got out, shouting and joking, swarming all over Dad's car, congratulating him.

I won't go into the victory celebration, though I will say that Wild Bill and his green Thunderbird didn't come back. And, as it turned out, the T-bird was never parked in front of Dad's house.

One other observation. Mom and John Bennett were the only ones who had stayed behind on the lot. I noticed Dr. Bennett craning his neck, trying to watch the race from his rear window, and it looked to me like he wanted to be out there with the others celebrating Dad's win. But Mom, once again sitting next to Dad's hot rod, was frowning and acting like nothing out of the ordinary was going on beside her window. Like she had come here for an after-school Coke, and all this foolishness going on around her was not going to interfere with her quiet, well-ordered life. She looked straight ahead and never once glanced at Dad or all the hullabaloo going on next to her. But John Bennett finally did get out of his car and go over to see Dad.

"Well, George," he said, "you sure put Bill in his place. Good job."

Dad glanced away from the others to Bennett. I could see by his expression that Dad respected Bennett, and he answered him with a straight face. "Thanks, Johnny."

Then Dr. Bennett walked away and Dad went back to yucking it up with his friends.

Mom, left behind in the car, scowled and kept staring straight ahead. When John Bennett returned, she didn't even look at him. Then I saw Dad's eyes slide over to Mom in the white Olds. But Mom ignored his attention. Bennett started his car, honked for the carhop, paid his bill, and drove away. I saw Dad watching them leave out of the corner of his eye.

Gail and I watched the kids milling around Dad. He was enjoying the attention he was getting, and Becky Steel was all over him, making sure she got her share, too.

Right about that time, I suddenly remembered where we were and realized how many hours had gone by. I glanced at my watch, then at my sister. "Gail! The time! We've got to get back before Mom and Dad think we're—" Then an absurd thought crossed my mind. I said to Gail, "How about if I just go over to that blond kid sitting in that hot rod and say to him, 'Hi, Dad. It's me, your son, Chris. Just thought I'd let you know that Gail and I are all right. We'll be right home just as soon as we stare at a picture of you and Mom and wish ourselves back into the future. Okay?' "

Gail nudged me, casting her eyes around. "Shhh.

42

You better keep your voice down or somebody's going to call the men in the white coats." She stood up. "Come on. Let's get going before something like that does happen."

We took off as fast as we could for the house.

Little did we know that we were in for still another shock.

CHAPTER SIX

Gail and I turned off Jefferson onto Elm, discussing all the incredible things we had seen, when we suddenly realized we were on the street where Dad had grown up. And just ahead was the house he'd lived in. It hit both of us at once. Inside that house our father's parents, Grandpa and Grandma Davenport—who, you might remember, had died in a horrible car accident when we were infants—were actually alive right now!

"Chris," Gail said flatly, "I want to see them."

"So do I," I agreed uneasily, hearing the fear in my voice. "But how?"

We thought about this problem for a minute as we continued walking slowly toward their house.

Gail suggested, "Why don't we knock on their door and ask directions to someplace. Anything. I have to see them before we go back."

Our dubious plan was settled. We walked up to the small brick house our dad had pointed out to us so many times, and stopped. My heart was pounding and my mouth was dry.

We were going to talk to the dead.

I nodded to Gail, and we forced our legs to move. We crept up the front steps and rang the doorbell.

We held our breath.

The door pushed open.

And there she was, unbelievable as it seemed: Grandma Davenport, alive and well.

She must have been around forty, with only a hint of gray in her hair. She was plump and healthy looking, and the paisley dress she wore looked like the one I'd seen her in in some of the old pictures in the attic.

She sang out to us, "Hello. Are you looking for Sonny? I'm afraid he isn't home yet." She adjusted her glasses and gave us a closer inspection. "I don't think I've seen you two around here before, have I?"

I stared at Grandma Davenport, trying to overcome the mixture of astonishment and joy I felt at seeing her. She blinked a few times at us as we stood before her, speechless. Then Gail stammered, "We—we're lost." She tried to collect herself. "We're looking for . . . Bugler's Market. We know it's around here somewhere."

Grandma Davenport frowned in thought. "Bugler's Market, you say? Hmmm. I don't recall ever hearing of such a place."

Gail ventured, "Is—is there anyone else here who could help us find it? We're new to this town and a little turned around."

Grandma smiled understandingly. "Of course," she nodded. "I'll get my husband for you. Why don't you two come in out of the cold. I do believe it's going to snow any minute now."

We followed Grandma into Dad's old house, feeling butterflies in our stomachs. She led us into the living room, where a man was kneeling on the floor, working on a radiator.

"Jim," Grandma said to him, "these children are new here. They're looking for someplace called Bugler's Market. Ever hear of it?"

Grandpa Davenport stood up. He was a little shorter than Dad, but the resemblance between father and son was uncanny; our middle-aged father in the future, and our middle-aged grandfather standing there before us, looked almost like one and the same person. "New here, eh?" He smiled. "When did you move in?"

"Yesterday," I lied. And to avoid any more questions, I asked, "Isn't Bugler's around here?"

"Bugler's Market?" Grandpa repeated, scratching the back of his neck. "Sorry, kids, I never heard of such a place in Summerville. And I've been here all my life."

Too late, I realized our mistake. Bugler's hadn't even been built yet!

I spoke up quickly. "Maybe we got the name wrong. Actually, any market will do. Is there one around here?"

"Sure," Grandpa replied. "There's the A&P two blocks down, going west. Just turn right when you hit the sidewalk. We do all our shopping there and they've got everything we ever needed."

"I'm sure that will do," I said. "Thanks."

Then Gail did something none of us expected. She stuck out her hand to Grandpa, saying, "Thank you very much, sir."

Grandpa, caught a little off guard, quickly wiped his hand on his pants, and shook Gail's hand. "Why, you're welcome, miss."

I knew why Gail was doing this. She wanted to touch Grandpa, because she would never have the chance again. So I did the same, saying thanks, while feeling Grandpa's warm, rough hand in mine.

"Anytime," he said to me. "Anytime."

We even did the same with Grandma, taking her by

surprise, too. "Well, now," she giggled, "it wasn't anything at all. Glad we could help."

Grandma walked us to the door and opened it. "Good-bye."

"Good-bye," Gail and I said, and walked down the porch steps.

Grandma glanced up at the sky. "Those are snow clouds up there. Looks like we'll have a white Christmas for sure."

The door closed behind us, and we walked down the street in stunned silence. Suddenly tears filled my sister's eyes. "Oh, Chris," she sniffled, "they were alive, my God, they were alive. And now we'll never see them again. What an awful thing it is to go back into the past."

"I know," I answered, my voice becoming tight, my own tears blurring my vision. "I know."

It seemed like a terribly long walk back home.

CHAPTER SEVEN

Remembering that we were, in 1955, no better than common housebreakers who could go to jail if caught, we sneaked back into the house carefully. Fortunately, no one saw us.

Gail and I were still so shaken up from our experiences that we had temporarily forgotten about being missed by our parents. But once we were inside the strange yet familiar house, the seriousness of the problem really hit me.

Now it was my sister's turn to hit the panic button. She looked a little pale. "Mom and Dad are probably worried to death about our being gone for so long. They may even have called the police! After all, they expected us to be home when they got back. And that was hours ago!"

I started feeling butterflies again. "Well, we'll just have to make up some kind of story, because they sure as heck aren't going to believe *this* one."

"What kind of story could we possibly tell them?" Gail asked.

"Good question. There's no point in sitting around trying to think of one. Let's just get the heck out of here. Come on. Let's go up to the attic and wish ourselves home."

We climbed the two flights of stairs and entered the

attic. Lying on a box were Mom's diary and the picture of our parents. Gail picked them both up, then studied the picture, shaking her head. "How in the world are they ever going to hit it off tomorrow after what we saw today? They're such opposites. Mom is so—I hate to say it—but she seems like such a prude. So stuck-up."

"And Dad is a total show-off," I added. "I can't believe what he did today. Grandstanding in front of everyone like that. My dad, the hotdogger. The drag strip king of Summerville. Mister Cool. Jeez!"

Then Gail said, "Aren't Mom and Dad lucky to have such sensible children who aren't like that?" We had to smile at each other, knowing that there was quite a bit of our young parents in both of us.

"Well," I said, "let's get going. Let's look at the picture and hope that—"

"The picture!" Gail exclaimed, frowning at it. "We didn't bring a picture of Mom and Dad as adults! How can we go back to 1983 with a picture taken in 1955?"

"Wait." I grabbed my wallet and dug out a picture of our parents that I had taken the week before with our Polaroid. They were standing—of all places—by the mantel in our living room. "There," I said, handing Gail the picture. "That should do the trick."

She held the two pictures side by side. "What did you do, sneeze when you took it? It's blurry."

"Don't complain. We're lucky we have this to go back on."

We both sat down on the hard wood floor. She held up the new picture, saying, "Okay. Let's stare at it just like we did with the old one. Stare at it, Chris. Stare . . . stare . . . stare. Wish yourself back to 1983. Back. Back home to our time. Wish harder . . . harder . . . harder. . . ."

We worked at it for five minutes, but nothing happened.

"Chris! What's wrong? It isn't working!"

"I don't know. Let's keep trying."

Ten more minutes went by. Fifteen. Still nothing. Gail's face drained to a frightened white. "What are we doing wrong?"

I thought about it for a moment. I was scared, but I tried not to show it. "You know what I think it is?"

"What?"

"I think we're afraid that we won't be able to come back once we return to the future."

Gail nodded twice. "You're right. I guess I'm not putting everything I've got into it. Not like I did before. I want to be sure we're going to be at Bradburn's tomorrow. I'm afraid to leave." She frowned. "But what are Mom and Dad going to think when we don't come home tonight? They'll think we were kidnapped or something! They'll have the police out looking for us! They'll—"

"Hold it, Gail. There's nothing we can do about that. We tried to go back, but we just aren't ready for it."

We let the enormity of our dilemma sink in. Tomorrow would be the most important day of our lives. And we were going to witness it—no matter what the consequences.

But, boy, were we ever going to pay the piper when we got back. Actually, we were paying for it already, just imagining what our parents were going through. It was a no-win situation. And neither of us could have imagined how much worse it was going to get.

We decided we had no choice but to spend the night in our house, even though it didn't belong to us. And even though we had no idea when the owners were coming back. We fixed ourselves some peanut butter and jelly sandwiches, turned off all the lights so the house looked empty, and turned on the black-and-white TV in the living room. It wasn't easy, thinking about our parents in the future probably going crazy trying to find us, and about our teenage parents meeting each other tomorrow and falling in love. Our brains were too overloaded and needed a shutdown. So we tried to lose ourselves in what is now called vintage television.

I discovered that in 1955 our town had only one channel, and you can forget about cable TV. But what was on—the old Westerns and comedies—was fun to watch. And some of it was a lot better than the stuff that's on TV today.

But none of it really helped very much. We kept thinking about our two sets of parents and what tomorrow would bring. And I can tell you that neither of us got much sleep that night.

CHAPTER EIGHT

We woke up to a cold, gray Christmas Eve morning. Gail and I had a breakfast of eggs and bacon and coffee, which we were lucky to find in the nearly empty kitchen. The house was warm—I had turned up the thermostat yesterday—and so we sat at the kitchen table discussing all that had happened, and what was about to happen.

"After yesterday," my sister said, "it seems incredible that anything is going to happen between Mom and Dad today. Yesterday she acted like she wouldn't even spit on him, much less become friendly with him."

"Maybe," I replied, finishing off my coffee with a bitter face, "it's because it's Christmas. You know how people get this time of year. Your way of thinking changes. People start liking each other."

"But Mom wouldn't even *look* at Dad," Gail said, her voice rising. "How is she ever going to fall in *love* with him?"

"Well, there are such things as miracles, you know. After all, we're here, aren't we?"

Later that morning we sneaked out of the house again around eleven o'clock and headed downtown for Bradburn's. Downtown was bustling with last-minute shoppers. People were bundled up in coats and hats and mufflers, their breath puffing out in frosty clouds. Children pulled at their mothers' coat sleeves, in a hurry to see Santa Claus ringing his bell in front of Bradburn's, or to catch one more glimpse of the traditional window display. Then, as now, the display was filled with mechanical elves working diligently with little hammers and saws in Santa's workshop. From the speakers outside of Bradburn's came the sound of Gene Autry singing "Rudolph, the Red-Nosed Reindeer" and "Jingle Bells." Everyone was toting packages, glancing up at the low gray sky, wondering when it would begin to snow, then turning around to greet some friend with a cheerful "Merry Christmas!"

Gail and I pushed through the thick glass front doors of Bradburn's to join the crowd of shoppers inside. Bradburn's was decorated with giant red ribbons, three-foot candles, and, in the middle of the store, a huge elevated Christmas tree loaded down with ornaments. Long lines of impatient customers stood at each cash register with their purchases. And the glass front and side doors never seemed to stop opening and closing.

"How are we ever going to spot Mom and Dad in all this mess?" Gail said as she scanned the crowd.

"Good question." I looked over the situation. "I'll tell you what. You stand by the side doors, and I'll take the front. The first one to spot them will go get the other. It's all we can do."

So we posted ourselves in our assigned places and waited.

As I watched the hordes of shoppers go by, I had time to think about some things that I hadn't thought of before. I began thinking about all the things these people hadn't lived through yet. Nineteen fifty-five seemed like such a nice year to live in. Oh, not that the country didn't have its problems then. I've read about the constant fear of the atomic bomb being dropped by Russia. And the paranoia about Communist spies trying to take over the U.S. That had everyone jumpy.

But just think of all the things they didn't have to worry about. These people could walk outside at night without any fear of being mugged before they got to the end of the block. And I don't think that many people worried about making their houses burglar-proof, as they do now. They didn't have to worry about their neighborhoods being used as chemical dumping grounds. And there weren't so many American families falling apart: kids turning their brains to mush with dope; teenagers running away; and one out of three couples getting divorced. Maybe I'm wrong, but it seemed like the country just wasn't as crazy as it is today.

As I looked at these people, I felt sorry for them, because some really bad stuff was down the road. Vietnam and violent antiwar demonstrations. Riots provoked by racial discrimination. Rampant crime. Immorality run amok (Mom's favorite saying). And all those assassinations. I mean, some really horrible things.

I wanted to warn these people of 1955. I wanted to tell them what was going to happen in the future so they would be outraged and try to prevent it all from coming true. But I knew it was all going to happen, no matter what I did. Anyway, who would believe me if I did tell them? Who would listen? I wished there were a way of changing the future; but, really, if one thing doesn't happen, doesn't another take its place? And who's to say the other thing won't turn out to be worse?

These thoughts were flooding my mind when Gail came running up to me. "Chris! It's Dad! He just came into the store. He's with Aunt Alice. And she's twelve years old!"

Dad's middle-aged sister, who has three kids of her own? Twelve years old? I wasn't sure I'd ever get used to being a time traveler.

"Where are they?"

Gail grabbed my arm and pulled me into the crowd. "Come on! Hurry before we lose them!"

We pushed our way along the aisles until we spotted Dad and his sister with a group of shoppers. They were watching a girl demonstrating a Hula-Hoop, which was all the rage then. They left the demonstration after about a minute, then meandered around the store, looking at things. We followed them, keeping one eye on Dad and another out for Mom. Our hearts were beating a mile a minute. The big moment was coming, and we were going to see it, actually *see* it happen!

We trailed Dad and Aunt Alice up to the second floor toy department, where the two of them stopped to watch a long line of small, nervous children waiting to talk to Santa. A little girl was on Santa's knee when we got there, and a store photographer was doing all sorts of things to get the kid to take the right pose for a picture. Santa was looking a shade weary, like he needed a lunch break. Dad and Aunt Alice watched the little girl squirming on Santa's lap, obviously thinking the whole thing was pretty funny.

That's when we spotted Mom and her mother—our years-younger grandma Gilbert—coming our way.

"Chris!" Gail whispered excitedly. "There's Mom!

And Grandma! This is it! I've got to get closer to hear what happens!''

Before I knew what was happening, Gail darted away from me. I dashed after her, running into people, trying to stop her. But I was too late. To my horror, I saw that in her excitement, she had gotten too close to where Dad was standing. Then, from out of nowhere, a woman chasing after her little boy ran smack into Gail, pushing her right into Dad, almost knocking him over.

At that same instant, Mom walked by, not noticing them. She dropped a package, stooped down, picked it up, and walked off with her mother toward the escalator.

Unable to move or think, I saw Gail face-to-face with our teenage father, as they both recovered from their collision. Dad frowned at Gail and was about to say something to her, but she recoiled in fright at what she'd done and, without losing another second, spun around and took off after Mom.

I managed to pull myself together enough to grab her and pull her away to where Dad couldn't see us. "Are you crazy?" I growled. "Now look what you've done!"

Gail tried to pull away from my grip on her arm. "Chris! Mom's getting away! I've got to stop her! Let me go! Let me go!"

"Shut up!" I said, trying to control her and myself at the same time. "It's too late! She's gone, and there's nothing we can do to stop her!"

We looked aghast at our teenage mother and her mother calmly getting on the escalator, descending out of sight.

Gail's eyes were wide with terror. "Chris! What have I done? I've ruined everything!" Her hands flew to me, her eyes swallowing up her face. "Oh, no! Worse than that! I've changed the past!"

For an instant, I was almost paralyzed. Gail tried to break away again. "I've got to stop Mom before she gets away!"

"And do what?" I exploded angrily, trying to keep my voice down. "Tell her you're sorry for getting in the way? That you're sorry you prevented her from meeting her future husband? Just what is it you plan on telling her, Gail?"

She looked around desperately. Dad and Aunt Alice were gone. A few people close by looked at us to see what was going on, then went on their way, going about their shopping as though nothing had happened. And for them, what had happened between Gail and our father and the careless lady *was* nothing. An insignificant incident inside a crowded store on a busy Christmas Eve. Only Gail and I knew its import. And we were scared to death.

As we walked out of the store, the Santa ringing the bell by the door wished us a merry Christmas. But Gail and I walked past him like two zombies. After a couple of blocks, Gail spoke in a shaky voice. "What's going to happen now, Chris?"

"I don't know."

"I've changed everything, haven't I?"

"I don't know."

"I've altered the past. I've ruined everything, haven't I?"

"I don't know."

"Stop saying 'I don't know'!"

But I didn't know what else to say. I was scared. Real scared.

Because a woman had run into Gail, Dad didn't see Mom drop the package he was supposed to have picked up. They were supposed to have talked, grown to like each other, fallen in love, dated, married, had us for children. But now the past had been interfered with. One thing probably would change another in a never-ending chain reaction. And now who knew what the future would bring?

Gail stopped and grabbed my arm, hard. She looked at me with a horrified expression. "Chris . . . If I prevented Mom and Dad from meeting back there . . . and if they . . . if they don't get married . . . then . . . doesn't that mean . . . that we were never born?"

I opened my mouth to reply, but nothing came out. I didn't have an answer.

CHAPTER NINE

We couldn't face going back to an empty house. The thought of sitting around the house—a house that didn't belong to us, in a world we didn't belong in—was too depressing. So we ended up walking around downtown for a while, wondering what to do next. But being surrounded by thousands of happy people buying presents for the ones they loved, smiling, laughing, greeting each other, didn't help at all. So we left the business area and walked through our old familiar neighborhoods, where we felt more despondent by the minute.

Gail kept blaming herself for what she'd done, until she got it out of her system and fell silent.

As we rambled down the tree-lined streets, I tried to think of what we could do to get ourselves out of this mess. But everything I thought of frightened me even more.

After walking for a long time, we stopped on the edge of Lewis Park and sat down on a wooden bench. The weather had turned colder and the sky grayer. I glanced down at my watch. It was a little after two in the afternoon.

"What are we going to do, Chris?" Gail moaned.

"How should I know? I'm not an expert at putting back together a fouled-up past." I pressed my lips shut and glanced sideways at my sister. She looked absolutely sick. "Sorry. I didn't mean that."

"I fouled everything up, all right. If it wasn't for that stupid lady who ran into me. That stupid, stupid lady!"

"Forget it. Let's just concentrate on what we can do to straighten this mess out."

A long moment went by. Then Gail said, almost hopefully, "What if—what if we tried again to go back to 1983? Right now. Maybe everything would be all right, and we could just forget this whole thing ever happened."

"You mean like stick our heads in the sand?" I replied. Then I added, in a kinder voice, "I've already thought about that. About going back."

"And?"

"And it scares the heck out of me."

"Why?"

"Because. If Mom and Dad never get married because of what happened in the store, then that brings up the question you asked: Were we ever born? And the only answer to that is no. How could we be? And, to tell you the truth, what I don't get is why we're still here at all. What I keep asking myself is, Why didn't we simply vanish the moment you ran into Dad and prevented him from talking to Mom? We changed Mom and Dad's past that very instant. And there are only two answers I can come up with."

"What?" Gail looked like her heart was going to stop.

"The way I figure it, either Mom and Dad are still going to get together sometime, somewhere, and fall in love and get married, and have us for their children, or . . ."

"Go on. Or what?"

I licked my lips, trying to think of how to put this. "Or we did alter the past, and they never will get married, and . . . we never will be born. And we're— I don't know—we're somehow alive and . . . not alive."

Gail's hand went to her throat. "What?"

"I mean, we existed in 1983, and we exist right now in 1955, and the laws of physics can't change that fact. But now the laws of time *have* been changed. If Mom and Dad didn't have us for their children, then we don't exist in time. But we do exist in space. I mean, here on earth. Now. I mean—Good Lord, I don't know *what* I mean."

"Chris, make sense."

"Maybe if I were Albert Einstein, I could." I tapped my finger against my mouth, thinking. "It could be that we're in a time zone no one has ever experienced. A fourth dimension. A sort of limbo between time and space."

"Then what you're saying is that we can't ever go back?"

"That's what scares me. We know we're alive now. But I think if we tried to go back to our time, especially after what's happened, then somewhere during the trip back we could very well . . . vanish."

"Vanish?" Gail choked.

"Because we couldn't exist in 1983 any more. Don't you see? Not if Mom and Dad never had us. We exist here, but not in the future. We were never born. Not you in 1968 or me in '67. And so we're stuck here, whether we like it or not."

"We can't ever go back?" Gail turned white as a sheet. "Oh . . . my . . . God!"

"Don't worry," I said, trying to sound confident. "We're not licked yet. We're still alive, and Mom and

Dad are still out there ready to meet each other. What we have to do is somehow glue things back together." I stood up with renewed determination. "Come on. Let's get going."

"But where to?"

"I'm not sure. All I know is, we're fighting for our very lives and we can't do it just sitting around here."

CHAPTER TEN

We started walking again, even though neither of us knew where we were going or what we were going to do. After we'd walked a couple of blocks, we heard the now familiar mufflers of Dad's hot rod behind us. We turned and saw him driving down the street with a girl sitting beside him and a Christmas tree sticking out of the rumble seat. As they drove past us, we saw that the girl was Becky Steel, and she had her arm around Dad's neck!

"Oh, no!" Gail howled, as we watched the roadster turn left at the intersection. "It's Mrs. McConnell! Dad's with *her* again!"

I was suddenly infuriated by all this mess. "Come on!" I shouted. "Let's hurry over to Dad's house. It's only a block away."

We ran down Ash Street to Elm just in time to catch everyone out in front of Dad's house. We ducked behind some evergreen bushes and peeked through the branches. Dad was untying the tree while Becky helped him. Grandma and Grandpa Davenport were walking out to the car with little Aunt Alice. Dad pulled the tree from the rumble seat and stood it up proudly on the curb for all to admire. It was a beautiful, full, seven-foot pine.

Gail looked away. I could barely hear her say, "Dad

was going to get a tree like that for us before we left home.'' Her voice quivered. ''And now we can't go back home. Oh, Chris—''

''Come on, Gail,'' I said slowly. ''Let's get away from here.''

But she didn't move. She turned back to watch, and I could see the tears sparkling in her eyes.

We heard everyone exclaim over the tree. Then Dad and Grandpa each took an end of it and carried it into the house, while the others followed behind.

The front door closed, leaving the sidewalk deserted.

Gail sniffled and wiped her nose with her handkerchief. ''That was supposed to have been Mom with Dad. The diary said that she went tree shopping with him on the day they met. Today. Now it's Mrs. McConnell who's taken Mom's place. She'll be the one to help him decorate it instead of Mom. It's all wrong now. The past is all—'' Then she gasped. ''What—what if Dad winds up marrying Mrs. McConnell instead of Mom? Then we—''

''—will never have been born,'' I finished. ''They'll have other children, not us.''

My sister's voice became small, her head bowed. ''Oh, Chris, what have I done? Why did I have to foul up everything? Why did I talk you into going into the past? Why?''

She looked like she was really on the way to a crying jag this time, and that I didn't need. So I said, ''Let's go by Mom's house. I can think better when I walk.''

Mom's house was on the opposite side of Lewis Park, on Jefferson Avenue. I didn't know what we would accomplish by going there. I just didn't want us to get any more depressed than we already were, and walking in the cold air at least kept me going. And Gail, too.

But that idea backfired, because parked out in front of Mom's house was John Bennett's white Oldsmobile.

Gail flew into a rage. "That does it! It's Christmas Eve, and Mom and Dad are with the wrong people! Everything's wrong! Wrong! Wrong!"

"Then we have to make it right," I said, glad to see my sister angry rather than teary-eyed.

"How?" she implored. "What can we do?"

"I don't know yet. But we'll think of something."

There was nothing to do but go back home.

CHAPTER ELEVEN

Gail and I fixed ourselves a dinner of beans and Spam, then washed it down with Kool-Aid. Needless to say, the half-empty cupboards were becoming bare. But we decided not to worry about what the present owners of our house would think when they came back and found their kitchen empty. There were more important problems on our minds.

Once again we turned off the lights in the house for fear of somebody calling the police. Wouldn't that have put the old frosting on the cake if we were arrested in our own house for breaking in? And think of the three-ring circus we would have caused trying to explain that our parents were two teenagers living in town and that we hadn't even been born yet (and maybe never would be). That would have put us on the Ripley's-Believe-It-Or-Not honor roll, all right.

The house had grown dark inside, and our mood was just as black. There was no way we were going to sit around watching TV again.

"Let's go," I said, getting up from the couch in the living room, where we had been talking.

"Where to?" Gail seemed as glad to leave as I was.

"Anywhere is better than here."

And so we bundled up against the falling tempera-

ture, helping ourselves to everything we needed from
the closets in the house.

"There's one thing we have to think about," I said,
as I put my muffler on. "If we get close to Mom or
Dad, we have to cover our faces with these. Otherwise they're going to remember seeing us in 1955. And
we'll never be able to explain that when we get back."

We headed down the dark streets of our neighborhood toward Mom's house. As we walked, I envi-
sioned everyone at home looking frantically for us.
Our pictures in all the newspapers and on TV, our de-
scriptions broadcast on every radio station. I saw police sending out all-points bulletins, combing the
neighborhoods, dragging the river for our bodies. I
imagined Mom and Dad, Grandpa and Grandma Gilbert, friends, neighbors—all of them searching for us
in the woods outside of town, hoping against hope that
they would find us alive.

I tried to block all that from my mind as we walked
down Chestnut, crossed under the street lamp at the
intersection, and turned onto Jefferson. We stopped
in front of Mom's two-story white frame house and
saw that Dr. Bennett's car was no longer there.

I told Gail, "I'm going to sneak up there and take a
look. Wait here."

I crept across the dark, shadowed lawn and peeked
in the window. There were Grandma and Grandpa
Gilbert, in their late thirties, sitting in the living room
listening to a radio program that sounded like the old
"Fibber McGee and Molly" show. She was curled up
on the couch under an afghan, knitting, while he sat
back in his easy chair, smoking a pipe and reading a
paper.

I crept back to Gail and reported, "Mom's not

there. At least, I didn't see her. Let's go by Dad's and check things out."

We cut through Lewis Park to Elm, then walked past a few houses to Dad's small brick house. Dad's hot rod wasn't parked out front. Again, I made my way across the yard to the window. It was eerie seeing Grandma Davenport sitting in her dining room. And, wouldn't you know it, she was listening to the same program. She sat at the table, polishing silverware and chuckling over something Fibber was saying to Molly. Loud, tinny laughter poured out of the old cathedral radio in the living room.

I went back to the sidewalk and told Gail, "Dad's not home, either. Just Grandma."

"So where is everybody?"

Then it dawned on us simultaneously. "Lewis Pond!" we said in unison, and headed across the street.

The people of my town have been going to Lewis Pond to ice skate at night ever since it was built at the turn of the century. Roger Lewis, who had a glove factory in town, loved to ice skate. He built the park, had it landscaped with pine trees, and put a circular, three-foot-deep pond in the center of the park. Then he ringed the pond with street lamps—gas back then— so the townspeople could skate at night after a hard day's work in his factory. And on each side of the pond he placed a large stone pit to build a fire in. Mr. Lewis died a long time ago, and his factory closed. But his pond and spirit still live on in Summerville.

It doesn't take a whole lot for the pond to freeze over, and it had been cold enough to put a good two inches of ice on the top. When we looked down Sledder's Hill at the pond, it looked just like it does in our own time. All the globes of the street lamps circling the pond were glowing. Two fires were crackling, shooting bright yellow and orange sparks into the freezing night air. There were around twenty skaters on the pond, scratching patterns on the ice with their blades. I could hear music down below. Someone had set up a portable radio on a picnic bench, and the sounds of Bing Crosby singing "White Christmas" floated dreamily over the park.

I checked the cars parked on the street; Dad's hot rod and John Bennett's Olds were among them.

Gail and I walked down the steps to the pond. She pointed her gloved hand toward the skaters moving in circles. "There they are. See?"

Sure enough, there was Dad, skating with Becky Steel, and Mom with Dr. Bennett.

A man near one of the fires called out to us. "Come on over, kids. There's room for everyone."

We strolled over toward him and the others. As we came closer, the man stepped into the light of the fire. It was Grandpa Davenport!

"Well, I'll be," he smiled. "You're the kids who were looking for that store." He stuck out his hand to shake ours, just like we'd done to him in his house. I guess he thought he should do it again just to be friendly.

It was Gail and I who were caught completely off guard this time. We quickly regained our composure, and both of us shook Grandpa's hand again, feeling his strong grip in ours.

"I'll introduce myself this time," Grandpa said. "Name's Jim Davenport. What's yours?"

I cleared my throat. "Hi, Mr. Davenport. My name's Chris . . . Edwards," I lied. "This is my sister, Gail."

"Hello, Gail. Find the A&P all right?"

"Huh? Oh, yes. We found it. Thanks again."

Grandpa smiled at us, looking us up and down. "Too bad you two didn't bring your skates. This is the first day the pond's been frozen solid this year."

I replied, "We just came over to check it out. But I guess we should have brought our skates."

"Well, you come back tomorrow. Everyone'll be here. Be a good chance for you to meet the folks here in town."

"That sound good," I answered. "I think we'll do that."

"Here," Grandpa said, handing us two opened coat hangers. "Roast yourselves some marshmallows. I brought plenty."

We thanked him and stuck marshmallows on the ends of our coat hangers, sidled up to the fire, and warmed ourselves at the welcome blaze.

Grandpa stuck his coat hanger in the flames next to ours. "It's good to have some new faces here in town. Where'd you two say you were from?"

I had to think fast. The first place that came to mind was a St. Louis suburb called Webster Groves, where my aunt Alice had moved when she got married. And just as I opened my mouth to say this, who should walk up to the fire but Aunt Alice herself! Only it was the twelve-year-old version we'd seen at Bradburn's yesterday.

"Webster Groves," I half choked, looking from Aunt Alice to Grandpa Davenport.

He was about to say something when he realized Alice had come up behind him. "Oh, kids, I want you to meet my daughter, Alice. Honey, this is Chris and Gail Edwards. They're new here in town."

I had already thrown my muffler over my mouth in

one swift move and kicked Gail on the foot to do the same. After all, what would our aunt Alice say when she remembered in 1983 about the night she was introduced to us back in 1955!

We said hi to one another and got down to the business of roasting marshmallows. The four of us made small talk about the weather and the good ice on the pond and about Christmas, and things like that. Gail and I kept our faces covered, except when we had to eat our blackened marshmallows. To do that we backed away from the fire, keeping our faces away from the light as best we could.

"That's my son over there in the white sweater," Grandpa said, pointing out our father. "He sure loves to skate fast, that boy. He insisted on coming over here just as soon as we'd decorated the tree and eaten dinner. He's just like me. People think we're daft, but we think winter's the best time of the year. Nothing like skating to lift a person's spirits and keep him young."

"Sonny likes to show off on the ice," Alice spoke up while munching. "One of these days he's gonna break his silly neck."

We all looked over toward the pond, and, sure enough, Dad was out there zipping around on the ice, cutting in and out of people, doing reckless turns and, in general, hotdogging it for everyone's benefit, just as he had done in his hot rod yesterday. A small crowd of his friends were whooping it up, encouraging him to make an even bigger ass of himself.

"Who's that with your brother?" I asked, just to open things up. "I think I saw her at the high school with him yesterday."

"Oh, that's Becky Steel," Aunt Alice answered. "She's one of the girls Sonny hangs around with."

"And who's that girl over there?" Gail asked, pointing to Mom as she skated by our side of the pond with Dr. Bennett.

"Her?" Aunt Alice said, sounding a little surprised that Gail would ask such a thing. "That's Liz Gilbert, the town pill."

"Now, honey," Grandpa said, "that's no way to talk."

"Well, she is. Thinks she's so smart because she always makes A's in school."

"And what's wrong with that?" Grandpa wanted to know. "You could use a few A's yourself, young lady."

"Oh, Daddy," Alice grumbled, a little embarrassed.

Then Gail asked Alice, "Why do you call her a pill?"

"Because," Aunt Alice replied, "my brother says she's one. All the kids do. She thinks she's too good for everyone."

"How's that?" Gail pursued.

"Oh, she's the uppity type. You know. She—"

"Now, now," Grandpa broke in. "These two are new in town, Alice. Let's not start gossiping about our own neighbors." He grinned at us. "You two will be going to the high school, and I'm sure you'll be forming your own opinions about your classmates soon enough. Now, then," he said, lacing his ice skates back on, "I think I'll take a few more turns on the ice before we head back home." He winked at Alice. "I'm sure your mother thinks we fell in."

He sailed away on the ice with the grace of a practiced skater, leaving us at the fire with Aunt Alice and five other people.

Gail didn't waste any time. "Tell me, why do you think Liz Gilbert's a pill?" she asked Alice again.

"Because she acts stuck-up to everybody."

"Everybody? Like to your brother?" Gail ventured.

The twelve-year-old girl looked at my sister, hesitated, then felt safe enough to answer. "Yeah. Like Sonny. She won't even look at him. I'm sure she thinks she's too good for him. At least he says she acts that way."

Gail pushed on. "Is Liz going with Doc—I mean," she quickly corrected herself, "with that guy she's skating with?"

"Johnny Bennett? Nah. They're just old friends. Nothing hot 'n' heavy there. They just have a couple of things in common—brains and money." Then Aunt Alice cocked her head at my sister. "Why are you so interested in all this, anyway?"

Gail shrugged innocently in the firelight. "Oh, just wondering, that's all. I like to get the low-down on people, to find out what's going on. Know what I mean?"

Alice thought about it for a second. "Yeah. I gotcha. I like to get the scoop on kids when I get in a new crowd, myself."

I decided not to interfere with them. Gail was doing too good a job for me to risk blowing it. So I walked casually around to the other side of the fire to roast another marshmallow. I kept my ears open, though, and heard Gail say next, "You said Becky Steel's your brother's girl friend? Are they going steady or anything?"

"Becky? Nah. She's not really Sonny's girl friend. I mean, he's not serious about her. She's pretty serious about him, though. Sonny has so many girl friends that he doesn't have time to get tied down to anybody. Anyway, he's always working on his car. That takes up most of his time. He's got a real neat hot rod. It's always falling apart, and he's always putting it back together. You know how that is."

Gail nodded. "You bet I do."

"Say," Alice suddenly piped up, "how about if I introduce you to Sonny? He might even ask you for a date."

Gail's eyes flew open in horror. The thought of Dad asking her out almost knocked her over. "No! I mean—that's all right. He's with Becky now. I wouldn't—"

"Yeah, I guess you're right. It wouldn't be too cool. Maybe some other time, eh?"

"Maybe." Gail recovered herself and ventured out a bit more. "Has your brother ever talked about going out with Liz Gilbert?"

Alice threw back her head and guffawed at that one. "Are you kidding? Liz is a big, A-One fruit. Sonny wouldn't go out with her if you paid him."

"Why do you say that?"

"'Cause. She's a drip. She's not his type. She's the kind who's always where everyone else is, but she never *does* anything. Know what I mean?"

"Yeah," Gail replied. "Sounds like she wants to be a part of things but doesn't know how."

"Maybe that's it. But no one can figure her out. I guess she's just too smart for the rest of us. Sonny calls her the Brain. Everyone does: the stuck-up Brain."

Gail glanced at Mom as she skated by, then looked back at Alice. "This Liz looks like a nice person to me."

"Maybe she is. Who knows? Not that many people are friends with her, so nobody knows her good enough to say."

Gail didn't want to press the matter, so she went back to stuffing her face with marshmallows, making small talk with Aunt Alice until Grandpa came back. I strolled around the fire and rejoined them, still keeping the muffler over my mouth.

Grandpa skidded to a stop at the edge of the pond, stepped on firm ground, and headed back toward us, smiling shamefacedly at himself. "Whew," he said to us. "Almost fell out there. Either I'm tired or my legs are getting old."

"Or," Gail said, "it could be because you haven't been skating for nearly nine months."

"Yeah, that must be it," Grandpa replied. "Or at least that's the excuse I'm going to use."

I joined in, saying, "You're a good skater, Gran—" Now *I* had to correct myself. "Mr. Davenport."

"There was a time when I was as good as Sonny. He's the champ now." He unlaced his skates, switching over to his shoes. "Well," he said to Alice as he stood up, "guess we better be going." Then to Gail, as he held out his hand to her, "Be seeing you, Gail. You drop by again next time you get lost, hear?"

My sister took his hand in hers. "I—I sure will, Mr. Davenport." She smiled bravely up at him.

Then he shook my hand for the last time. "See you, Chris. I hope you like our town. It's a good place to live in."

"I know I'll like it," I replied. "Good-bye."

We watched the father and daughter climb the stone steps going up the side of Sledder's Hill and disappear over the rim into the darkness.

Gail turned to me, pulling down her muffler, a look

of sadness clouding her face. "Oh, how I wish Grandpa had lived. He's such a nice man. Think of all we missed, not having him with us."

I felt a lump rising in my throat. "Yeah, I know."

"Well," Gail sighed, "at least we had the chance to know them for a little while. At least we had that much."

That was the thing about going back in time. There were so many good things you could do, like see people you would never see otherwise, actually talk to people who were dead. It was scary—but it was wonderful, too.

CHAPTER TWELVE

We watched Mom skating on the ice with Dr. Bennett for a minute. The light from the lampposts plated the surface of the pond in soft silver. They moved over the ice slowly, etching it with their blades, making patterns, talking to each other in low voices.

I felt myself getting angry again. Why wasn't that my father skating with Mom? Why John Bennett? For one foolish moment, I was jealous of Dr. Bennett. But then I remembered that he was only a friend of Mom's—and, later, a good friend of Dad's. All three had grown up together, and my parents and Dr. Bennett and his wife go out on Saturday night all the time. They visit each other's houses and play golf and bridge together. I had to keep telling myself that what was happening now would change in the future. But how?

There was Dad, streaking around the pond at breakneck speed, yelling and making all sorts of noise to attract attention. Becky Steel had long since stopped trying to keep up with him and was standing by the other fire with a small group of kids who were calling out to Dad, egging him on to try all sorts of death-defying feats.

For a moment, I was half tempted to run out there and give my teenage father a good punch on the nose and tell him that he'd better shape up and start skating with Mom. But, of course, that was not only absurd, it was dangerous. The past, I found out, is a very shaky house of cards: One slip and the whole thing can come tumbling down.

Or was it that fragile? I suddenly asked myself. Maybe that was the problem. What it really needed was a good kick in the pants.

That's when I formed my push theory, which I explained to my sister. "All right, listen up and tell me what you think of this. You accidentally pushed Dad away from Mom at Bradburn's, right?"

She gave me a tired, half-hearted smirk. "Is this meant to make me feel good? I know what I did. You don't have to rub it—"

"No, no," I interrupted quickly. "Just listen. Since you pushed Dad *away* from Mom, then why don't we fix it by pushing Dad *into* Mom? Maybe that's what we need to change things back to the way they're supposed to be."

"You mean you're going to go out there and . . .?" She stared at me, her pretty green eyes growing wider. "Are you insane?"

"You got a better idea?" I asked.

"No," she admitted. "But—"

"Then here goes," I said, and headed for the pond before she could stop me.

I wasn't sure exactly what I was going to do. All I knew was that doing anything would be better than doing nothing.

I watched Mom skate past me, almost close enough to touch her. It hit me again how young—so terribly, unbelievably young—she was. This was the girl who gave birth to me. And changed my diapers and taught me how to eat with a fork and spoon. This was the girl who spanked me when she caught me putting my socks in the goldfish bowl.

Then I watched Dad go sailing by, his skates hissing on the ice. And this was the boy who taught me how to ride my bike. Who put me on his shoulders and galloped me around the house when he came home from work. Who let me hide in bed with him during electrical storms.

These were my parents! And here they were skating around, hardly aware of each other!

Gail was scared, but I was angry. Real angry!

I pushed my muffler back over my nose and ventured out onto the ice, hoping no one would notice me—especially Mom and Dad. I was ready to risk everything on this one shot and I had to time it exactly.

Dad was making two trips around the pond for every one of Mom's. I waited several minutes, hoping they would somehow synchronize and pass me at the same precise moment. Finally, I saw my chance. I estimated their distances and rates of speed. There was no time to think it through. I had to do it now or lose my chance. I pushed out hard onto the ice and nudged Dad with what I thought was just enough force to cause him to bump into Mom as she skated by. Only the nudge turned out to be more like a ram, and the next thing I knew Dad collided with Mom, sending her sprawling on the ice with a yelp.

"You clod!" she screamed at Dad as she lay on her side, holding her knee in obvious pain. "Why don't you watch where you're going!"

Dr. Bennett, who'd almost been knocked over himself, skated back around, skidded to a stop, and bent over to help Mom up.

Dad had managed to keep his balance, and now he

made a wobbly circle and came back to where Mom was lying. "Me!" he shouted with indignation. "*There's* the clod over there!" He pointed an accusatory finger at his future son, as I apologized, hastily backing off the ice.

"I'm sorry," I said in my most sincere voice. "I lost my balance and I accidentally—"

"Oh! Ow!" Mom yelled, as Dad and John Bennett helped her to her feet. Then she snapped at Dad. "If you didn't rip around here like an idiotic show-off, you wouldn't crash into people!"

"Show-off!" Dad gasped, letting go of Mom. "I like that! That clown over there ran into *me*! Go yell at him!"

Mom fired back, "You skate the same way you drive that stupid car of yours, like a crazy hot rodder!"

Dr. Bennett tried to calm her down. "Come on, Liz. Take it easy. It was just an accident."

But Mom wasn't listening to him. "Crazy hot rodder!" she shouted at Dad again.

Dad had his hands on his hips, looking more hurt than mad. "Hot rodder? Just 'cause you and Bennett skate like refugees from a geriatric ward doesn't mean I have to mope around on the ice like an old man!"

"Come on, George," John Bennett said, trying to calm Dad down, too. "It's no big deal. It wasn't your fault."

But Mom wouldn't let it end there. "It doesn't surprise me that a big baby like you would regard responsible people like us as being *older* than you!"

Dad looked like Mom had just hit him. "What! Are you kidding me?"

"Oh, go back to your friends and show off for

them!" Mom barked. "You never impressed *me* with
your skating—or with that ridiculous thing you pass
off as a car!"

All Dad could choke out was another "What!"

Dr. Bennett started leading Mom away, but it was
obvious that she still wasn't finished. She brushed his
hand aside, scowling at Dad. "Grow up, Davenport!
We all have to sometime!"

I could see by Dad's expression that he was totally
crushed by Mom's attack. Without a parting shot, he
skated back to the other side of the pond and walked
over to the fire where his friends were waiting for him.
He jerked off his skates, put on his shoes, and left with
Becky—who looked flabbergasted by the whole thing.
A minute later, Gail and I heard Dad's car roar to life
and burn about forty feet of rubber up Elm Street.

Meanwhile, Mom and Dr. Bennett came over to the
fire where Gail and I were standing. We immediately
backed off into the shadows of a nearby clump of
pines and listened. Mom started jerking off her skates
in a fury. She was mumbling angrily to herself as she
threw one skate on the ground.

"Why were you so tough on George?" John asked,
as he started taking off his skates. "It was just an accident, you know."

"Because he's an idiot!" my mother snarled, her
green eyes flashing in the firelight. "He thinks he's so
cool, like James Dean or Marlon Brando. Always acting like the mixed-up kid who has to go after thrills
because he doesn't know what else to do!"

I saw John Bennett back up a couple of inches with
a surprised smile on his face. "Wow. That was a
mouthful. I've never heard you get so angry over
something so—"

"Forget it! Just forget it!"

A minute later they disappeared up the hill. We heard one car door slam louder than the other in the distance, then the sound of the Olds as it drove away.

"Now everything's *really* ruined!" Gail almost sobbed.

"Don't be so sure," I said. "I mean, I got Mom and Dad to talk to each other. That's something, isn't it?"

"They weren't talking to each other," Gail almost shouted. "They were *yelling*! Oh, they'll never fall in love now! Never!"

"All right," I said. "All right. We'll think of something else. Don't worry, will you?"

"*What* something else, Chris? Come on, tell me! You're the one with all the bright ideas!"

"I don't know!" I yelled back, suddenly losing my temper, too.

Then Gail threw her arms around me, her voice sounding small and frightened. "Oh, Chris, I'm sorry. I know you're trying to fix things up. I know we have to keep trying. We can't give up. We just can't."

"We won't," I whispered, as I patted her on the back. "We'll think of something."

Gail was right, of course. I didn't get our parents to talk to each other; I got them to yell at each other. Yet, it was a beginning. At least they recognized each other's existence. And I had a feeling that Mom's fury was a positive thing. I mean, if she wasn't interested in Dad, why didn't she just ignore him? Anyway, Gail and I were still here, weren't we? That meant there was still a chance that we could get our parents back on the right track. But if we couldn't . . .

I knocked the idea around with my sister as we sat by the fire, watching the skaters go around on the pond. "Don't you see? What if there's a point in time when the chances of Mom and Dad ever getting married will fall to zero? When their getting together will become an absolute impossibility? What will happen to us at that point? Will we disappear, or what?

"Oh, Chris." Gail shuddered. "Don't talk like that. I'm frightened enough as it is."

"But," I added quickly, "don't you understand what that means? If such a point does exist, then it hasn't been reached yet. There must still be a remote chance that Mom and Dad will get married in the future. There must be a chance that they'll have us as their children. And that's what's keeping us alive."

"I'm sick of theories," Gail moaned. "I just want to go back to our time and our parents and our home and forget this whole nightmare. Let's at least *try* to go back. I don't think I can take any more of this, Chris."

"We *can't* go back without knowing if we're going to be born. Don't you realize what could happen? We could disappear during the trip. Vanish on the way back to 1983. Are you willing to take that kind of chance? I'm not."

"But what if your theory about our disappearing is wrong? What if your idea is just a lot of science fiction hogwash?"

I waved my hand around us, indicating the park and the people and the world of 1955. "Do you call *this* a lot of science fiction hogwash? Do you think we're dreaming all this?" I closed my mouth because some people were starting to look at us. "Come on," I said, lowering my voice. "Let's move away from here." I led my dejected sister away from the fire over to one of the lampposts by the edge of the park.

Gail stood looking at the ground. I could see that she was going under. She had always been a pretty strong person, but now she was having a hard time holding herself together. All I could do was try to keep her from falling apart completely. I could just see her walking into a police station and telling them the whole story, hoping they could somehow fix the whole mess.

Gail kept staring blindly at the ground, appearing very small and lost. I put my arm around her shoulder and gave her a brotherly squeeze. "Don't worry. Everything's going to turn out all right."

"No, it's not," she said flatly. "We both know that now. I've made a complete disaster of this whole thing, and now we're going to pay for it for the rest of our lives. It's all my fault."

"It's *our* fault. I'm as much to blame as you. After all, I'm the one who brought up this time travel stunt in the first place. Remember?"

"Maybe you're right," she said, but not too convincingly. "We never should have interfered with the past. Even God doesn't do that. He . . ."

I saw Gail's expression changing. Like she had been searching for something for a long time and suddenly had found it. She looked up at me with a light in her eyes. "Chris? I want to go to church and pray. It's our only hope. No one can help us now except God."

She was right, of course. There wasn't anyone we could go to for help. We were more alone than we ever had been in our lives.

"All right," I said, as we started to leave the park. Then a thought popped into my head. "Hey. Why don't we talk to Father Ryan? Maybe he could help us?"

"Is he there now?" Gail asked hopefully. "Remember what year this is."

I couldn't figure out if Father Ryan was at our

church in 1955 or not. He had been there for as long as I could remember, but that didn't mean anything.

"I don't know, but there's only one way to find out."

We crossed the street and headed down Elm toward our church.

CHAPTER THIRTEEN

The familiar grade school—to which Gail and I had gone—and the connecting church of Christ the King, with its great stone spire, loomed ahead of us in the night. We walked to the tall front doors of the church and looked up. The large gold cross atop the spire was silhouetted against the dark winter sky. It was Christmas Eve, and we remembered that long ago two other people were alone on a cold night, seeking help. Well, Gail and I knew what being cold and lonely and afraid were all about. This was our last hope; our final stopping place before we—what?—gave up? No! We weren't going to do that. But whatever help we were going to find, we would have to find it here.

We walked in, both of us immediately feeling the comfort and security of the church's surroundings. In a way, it was a little like going home.

It was after ten, and in a Catholic church on Christmas Eve, that meant everyone was getting ready for midnight Mass. And our church was no exception. A boys' choir was practicing Christmas carols in the front of the church. A priest stood before them, waving his short arms in time with the music as he directed them. He was a small, dumpy, white-haired man, with an Irish face that held a mixture of whimsy and kindness. He stood before the dozen boys, nodding, saying gently to them, "That's it, boys, better, much better." His bushy white eyebrows seemed to be permanently arched upward and his lips, silently miming the words along with the shrill voices of the choir, were always on the verge of a smile.

I recognized Father Dooley immediately.

But then, that wasn't too hard to do. After all, a painting of him had been hanging in the entrance to our school as long as I could remember. Those cheerful, understanding blue eyes with the laugh wrinkles around them—so well captured by the artist—had suddenly come to life. The ready smile in the painting was now formed in real flesh. Yes, it was Father Dooley, all right. Father Dooley, who had died thirteen years ago, was once again a living, breathing priest in charge of Christ the King.

After Gail and I crept into one of the back pews and knelt down, I tapped her on the arm and pointed toward the old priest. She recognized him at once. "It's Father Dooley!" she whispered excitedly. "He's alive!"

"I know. It's so hard to believe."

"Let's go talk to him, Chris. Maybe he can do something to help us."

"No. Not yet. Let's wait till he's finished."

We closed our eyes and started praying, as we had done a thousand times when we were children and believed that praying for things helped you get them. I guess Gail and I had grown a little cynical in our teenage years. But right now we felt like terribly small and frightened children, and even the act of praying gave us hope. I looked at my sister kneeling beside me. Her eyes were shut tight, her forehead wrinkled in deep concentration. I noticed how white her knuckles were as she clenched her hands together in silent prayer. I closed my eyes again and leaned over the pew in front of me, resting my weary head on my folded hands, praying.

Suddenly, I felt something odd happening to me. All through me. Like I was going hollow. Empty. I gripped the pew with both hands and held on, because I felt so strangely light that I thought I was actually going to float away from the floor! I turned to Gail to say something and found her staring wide-eyed at me.

"Chris!" she gasped. "What's happening to me? I feel so . . ." Her eyes and mouth locked open in horror.

I stared at my sister, not believing what I saw. She started losing color, becoming translucent. Her clothes, too. I stared at her large, fearful eyes and thought I was losing my mind—because I was looking *through* them. I was looking through *her*! Unbelievable as it was, she was slowly disappearing.

That was when my hands started going through the wood of the pew I was holding onto. *Because I was disappearing, too!*

"Chris! What's happening! Oh, God, save us, we're disappearing! Please, God, help us, don't let this happen. Help us. . . ." Her fingers reached out again, clawing through me desperately.

And then, just as suddenly as it had begun, the feeling went away. We became solid again.

Gail and I blinked at each other, reading the fear in each other's faces. Then her eyes closed as she moaned and fainted dead away.

The next thing I knew, somebody was standing over us.

"What is it?" a man asked. "What's wrong? What's happened here?"

I looked up at the saintly face of Father Dooley. "It's my sister. She's fainted."

But before I could say anything more, Gail's eyes fluttered open. She looked around, confused, disoriented. Then her eyes settled on me. "Chris? Are we . . . alive?"

"Sure we're alive," I said, flashing her an oversized smile. "Everything's fine." But inside I was shaking all over.

Gail lifted her head a little, blinking herself back to reality. "Then we didn't disappear?" She searched me with her eyes. "Chris! We're still here!"

Now, while Gail and I were saying all this nonsense, there stood Father Dooley with a completely baffled expression on his face. "What did you say?" he asked, quickly sliding into our pew. "Now, now. What's this? What's this about being alive?"

In one move, Gail left me and slid over to Father Dooley. She actually buried her face against his shoulder, clutching his arm tightly. "Oh, Father," she pleaded, "please, you've got to help us."

"There, there, child," Father Dooley said, patting her on the shoulder, while giving me a puzzled look.

But I was in a state of shock myself, and when I tried to speak, I ended up sounding like a gibbering idiot. "I—I—I'm sorry, Father. We—we—you see, we're . . ."

"Now, now, that's all right," Father Dooley said to me. His eyes darted from Gail to me, then to the boys' choir, where a nun had taken his place. All of them had stopped what they were doing and were staring with keen interest at us. "Tell you what," the priest said. "Why don't you both come into my office, and you can tell me all about it there. Come on. Here we go. That's it."

He helped Gail down the aisle while I followed. An elderly nun in full habit came rushing toward us. Father Dooley whispered to her to continue the rehearsal, explaining that he'd be right back. The nun eyed us questioningly, then nodded to Father Dooley, saying, "Yes, Father." Then the priest led us to the back of the church, through a doorway leading to the rectory and into his office, where he closed the door behind him. He offered each of us a seat and took the chair behind his desk. For a moment he blinked at us, then gave us a reassuring smile. But Gail and I were so miserable that there was no way we could smile back.

"Now, then," he began, "why don't we start from the beginning. My name's Father Dooley. What's yours?"

I cleared my throat and spoke up. "I'm Chris Davenport, and this is my sister, Gail."

"Well, then, Chris and Gail," he said, his fingertips touching, his concerned eyes on us. "What seems to be the trouble with you two? What happened back there? You gave me quite a start."

I opened my mouth, but once again the only thing that came out was, "I—I—"

But Gail managed to blurt out, "Father Dooley! We're going to die! You've got to save us!"

The smile on Father Dooley's face fell. "What are you saying, child?"

Then Gail started jabbering away so fast, punctuating her words with such an assortment of hiccups, sniffles, and occasional sobs that even I couldn't understand what she was saying.

"There, there," the priest said. "Slow down, child, slow down." He got up, went into a connecting bathroom, and came back with two glasses of water. He handed us the water and waited until we'd gulped it down.

"Now, then," he said. "What's all this nonsense about you dying?"

"Father," I said, finding my natural voice at last, trying to look the priest in the face. "Let me start by saying that my sister and I are in serious trouble. I don't mean," I added quickly, "that we broke any laws or that we did anything wrong. Not that kind of trouble."

"Then what kind of trouble?" he wanted to know.

I looked at the small man in black, opened my mouth to speak, closed it with a sigh, then opened it again and said, "You won't believe me, Father."

"How can I believe anything if you don't tell me?"

"All right, Father. I'll tell you everything. I only hope you do believe us, because I think you're our only hope."

Father Dooley rubbed his chin. His wrinkled face was filled with interest and encouragement. "Go on, young man. Go on. I'm listening. Just start from the beginning."

I cleared my throat, adjusted myself in my seat, glanced over at Gail—who was watching me with desperate eyes—then turned back to Father Dooley and started my story from the beginning.

I was halfway through—at the part where Gail and I were meeting our dead grandparents—when Father Dooley, who had been listening to me without interruption, waved his hand at me to stop. "My boy," he broke in, "I don't know why I've been listening to you so long, except that your story is one of the most interesting and inventive fabrications I've ever heard. It's sheer nonsense."

That really made Gail's back stiffen. "Chris, show him the picture in your wallet. *That* should prove we're telling the truth."

I took the Polaroid snapshot out and handed it to Father Dooley. He studied it for a moment, then looked up at us. "So?"

"Those are our parents," I said, trying to control my temper. "Can't you see? That's George Davenport and Elizabeth Gilbert in that picture. Just add twenty-eight years on to them. Can't you recognize them?"

Father Dooley gave the picture one last hard look, then handed it back. "I don't see anything except a fuzzy picture of two adults who look like a hundred other people I know." He gave out an extra loud sigh and shook his head. "I don't know why you're doing this to me. I mean, why did you pick *me* for your prank? Really! Telling me that George Davenport is your father and Elizabeth Gilbert your—" Then his sharp eyes narrowed on me. "Did George Davenport put you up to this? If he did I'll get to the bottom of it with a phone call to his father, I can assure you of that!"

I opened my mouth to say something in my defense as he stood up.

"Really!" he scolded us. "This isn't Halloween. This is no night for tricks. I've got things to do. I must prepare for Mass. I've got the choir and other things to attend to. I must ask you both to go home now and not bother me any more."

"But, Father!" Gail exclaimed. "Everything my brother told you is true! We don't *have* a home to go to! We don't have parents to go home to! We're alone! Don't you understand? We're alone!"

Father Dooley stared down at my sister for an indecisive moment, then slumped back into his chair, not knowing what to do or say. "You're telling me you're both from the future—the year 1983—and you expect me to believe such foolishness?"

"But it's true!" Gail insisted.

Father Dooley shook his head, unable to believe what was being asked of him. His clear blue eyes suddenly bore down on my sister. "Then you'll have to come up with something more convincing than that," he said, pointing to the snapshot in my hand.

Gail and I glanced at each other nervously.

"Go on," the priest demanded, almost playfully. "If you're from 1983, then prove it. Pull out some ray gun and make my desk disappear."

I frowned. "There is no such thing as a ray gun, Father. I'm not talking about some Buck-Rogers-science-fiction-futuristic 1983. It's not that way at all. In fact, the future's not all that much different from the present. The only real change in Summerville is in the cars. And there are a few new buildings and houses around. Other than that, it looks about the same."

"Hmmm." Father Dooley looked a little disappointed in me, as though my capacity for far-fetched fantasy was suddenly running low.

And just at that moment I thought of my watch. "Here, Father, look at this. This should prove to you that we're from the future." I took off my new quartz digital watch with a minicalculator built into it. I demonstrated how it worked and watched as the priest's eyes widened in awe.

"Where—where did you get this?" he demanded.

"From Target. That's a discount store that hasn't been built yet. It's going to be put up on Dickerson's meadow."

Father stared at my watch as though it were the

eighth wonder of the world. "Why, this is the most amazing thing I've ever . . ." He forced his attention away from my watch and cast another narrowed eye on us. He regarded us for what seemed an eternity. Then he abruptly shot a question at me. "Who's the mayor of our town?"

I was caught off guard, but I suddenly realized what he was up to. "Mr. Banner's the mayor. Ed Banner."

"No, he's not," he corrected me. "It's Raymond Farley."

"But," Gail said, "Mr. Farley died a long time ago."

The next question was directed at Gail. "What's the name of the pope?"

"John Paul the Second of Poland," she replied.

Father Dooley hesitated, frowned, then continued. "Who's the governor?"

"Christopher Bond."

"Name a senator from Missouri."

"John Danforth," I piped up.

"Who's the president?"

"Ronald Reagan."

"Whaaat!" Father Dooley leaned all the way over his desk at me. "You don't mean the actor!"

"Yes, Father," I replied reluctantly, realizing I sounded like a complete idiot.

Father Dooley threw his head back and let out a long belly laugh that turned his pink face red. "Ronald Reagan! President! Oh, my boy, my dear boy, that *is* rich." And he laughed all over again. Then he settled down and leaned over, looking directly at me with a twinkle in his eyes. "Why are you doing this to me, Chris? Be honest now. I mean, I enjoy a good joke as much as anyone, but where did this one come from?"

"What do you mean, Father?"

"This prank you're pulling on me. Is it some kind of dare? Did George Davenport—or someone who's mad at him—put you up to this? Or have you seen so many science fiction movies that it all sort of went to your head?"

I was about to answer when Gail blurted, "If Father Ryan were here, *he'd* listen to us!"

Those words hit Father Dooley like a bomb. "*Father Ryan!*" His eyes widened. "How—how did you know about Father Ryan?"

Gail answered, "Because he's the pastor of this church."

Father Dooley frowned and turned a little pale. "*I'm* the pastor of this church! How did you know about Father Ryan? How?"

I shrugged my shoulders and replied, "Like my sister said, he's our pastor. He has been all our lives."

"But," Father Dooley stammered, "but—he's not even here yet! He's not supposed to arrive until next month!" He fished through some papers on his desk, then pulled out a letter, holding it up. "I just found out about it today! I didn't know a Father Ryan was being assigned to this parish until this afternoon's mail arrived! And I haven't told anybody! So how did you find out?"

"Father Dooley," I said calmly, realizing I was finally getting the upper hand, "Father Ryan baptized Gail and me. He's been in charge of this church all our lives."

"And what about me?" Father Dooley fired back. "I'm the pastor here."

"But you're—" I bit my lip to stop my words.

Father Dooley leaned over, scrutinizing me. "I'm *what*?" he said, his eyes fixing on mine.

"Not here any more." I lowered my eyes to the floor.

"You mean, I'm *dead*!"

All I could do was shrug and squirm in my chair.

The priest ran a nervous hand over his mouth. "And when did I—No! Don't answer that!" He looked around the room in disbelief. "What am I saying? Now you're getting *me* to believe all this nonsense." He pointed a shaky finger at me. "How did you find out that Father Ryan was being sent here? Who told you?"

"No one told me, Father. I've known Father Ryan all my life."

Just then there was a knock at the door. A different nun poked her head in, saying, "I'm sorry to disturb you, Father, but the time . . ."

Father Dooley looked up at the intruder and blinked. "Time? Oh, yes, of course, Sister. The time." He checked his watch, glanced uneasily at the high-tech one on my wrist, then forced his eyes back to the door. "Thank you, Sister. I'll be there in a moment."

The door closed quietly.

Father Dooley thought about the two of us for a few seconds, as though trying to make up his mind. Then he said, "I don't know what you two are up to, and I don't know how you learned about Father Ryan coming here, but . . . ." His eyes darted from me to Gail and back to me. "I'd like you both to come back here tomorrow after morning Mass. If your parents won't mind," he added, studying us for a reaction.

"Father," I replied, "our parents are two teenagers who don't even know us."

He stood up and came around his desk. "I don't have more time for this foolishness."

Gail and I rose to go.

"Has our country had any more wars since Korea?" he fired at me.

"Yes, sir," I replied, ready this time. "Vietnam."

"Never heard of such a place. Who's going to be president after Eisenhower?"

"John F. Kennedy," Gail said. "But he was assassinated."

He turned to Gail. "Assassinated!" He blinked at her for a moment, then asked, "And after this Kennedy?"

"Lyndon B. Johnson."

"After him?"

"Richard Nixon. But he quit."

"Quit? What do you mean, quit?"

"They were going to impeach him, and he quit before they did."

Father shook his head like he was trying to clear it from so much insanity. "Richard Nixon is our vice-president. I hope you know that, young lady."

"Yes, sir," Gail said firmly, "but he made some bad mistakes when he was president."

Father Dooley squinted at my sister. "And who comes after Nixon?"

"Gerald Ford finished Nixon's term."

"Then?"

"Jimmy Carter."

"*Jimmy* Carter?"

"That's what he wanted everyone to call him. He was a good old country boy. A peanut farmer from Georgia."

"After him?" Father went on, his voice beginning to sound very strange.

"Ronald Reagan."

"And who comes after him? Henry Fonda? John Wayne? Marilyn Monroe?"

"I doubt it, Father," I replied. "They're all dead now."

That stopped him cold. A sad expression crossed his face. Then he shook his head, as though trying to get rid of some troubling thoughts. "All right. All right," he said, ushering us out of his office. "Come back at eleven tomorrow morning. I don't know why I want to pursue this nonsense any further, except . . ." He gave Gail and me a strange, thoughtful look. "Except that you might . . ." His voice trailed off.

I finished the sentence for him. "That we might be telling you the truth?"

He raised his bushy eyebrows at me and said, "Nonsense." But it lacked conviction.

He walked us back into the church where the boys' choir was still practicing Christmas carols.

"Are you two staying for Mass?" he asked us. "Or do you have to get back home?"

Gail and I looked at each other and sighed.

"All right, all right," Father Dooley said. "I promise I won't try to trick you any more. Tomorrow at eleven."

And with that, he left us, hurrying off to prepare for midnight Mass.

Gail turned to me. "He doesn't know what to believe, does he?"

"Would you?"

"I guess not."

"But I think he's starting to believe us. We gave him a lot to chew on."

"At least we've got someone who will listen to us." Then Gail thought of something. "You don't think he'll have the police here when we come tomorrow? He wouldn't have us arrested or anything like that?"

I shook my head. "No. I think he wants to hear

more from us. I think we've got someone who's going to help.''

We stepped out into the cold night air and began walking home. My sister and I were mentally and physically exhausted, but we still had one more thing to talk about before this night was over. A subject we hadn't discussed with Father Dooley because it was so incredible.

Gail was the first to bring it up. "Chris? That thing that happened to us back at church.''

"Yeah.''

"You were right.''

I knew what she was talking about and kept on walking, thinking, worrying.

"We were vanishing. It almost happened.''

"I know.'' Just the thought of it made me sick.

"We were actually disappearing,'' Gail said, almost tonelessly. "I'll never forget how you looked . . . actually seeing through you like that. I thought for sure we would—''

"We can't worry about that now,'' I broke in. "We're here. Alive. We made it. That's all that matters.''

"But—for how long? It could happen again. We could go at any time.'' She hesitated. "What I don't understand is why we *didn't* completely disappear.''

I'd been puzzling over that same question. "There's only one thing I can think of. Mom and Dad must have been thinking about each other at the moment we went into church. And at that same exact moment they both must have decided they would never have anything to do with each other again. They must have written each other off as lost causes simultaneously. That was the point I was talking about. The point at which there wouldn't be any hope of them getting together. That's when we started to go.''

''Then what happened? Why are we still here?''

''I guess because after they thought about never having anything to do with each other''—I had to smile—''they must have changed their minds.''

''You mean they almost *thought* us away?''

''Not quite like that. But, yeah, that must have been what happened.''

''That's impossible,'' Gail said flatly.

''Oh, really? Didn't we wish ourselves into the past? Gail, we're fooling around with time, not the normal world. Anything's possible. There are a million things that could happen to us that we couldn't begin to imagine. We're in a twilight zone. A real one.''

There was a long silence between us as we walked down the dark street. We had both had it for one night.

''We'll get some sleep and feel better in the morning. You'll see.''

Then I thought: if we ever see morning.

CHAPTER FOURTEEN

You never really appreciate what you've got until you lose it. How many times have you heard people say that? Well, let me tell you, it's true. If there's anything I learned from this whole ordeal, it's that.

Imagine waking up Christmas morning without your parents because they're far away from you—not in miles, but in years. Twenty-eight years, to be exact. Imagine that you may never get back to them, that you're stuck where you are and don't know if you'll ever see them again. Then think of the agony your parents must be going through that same Christmas morning, because you're missing and they don't know where you are. And, worst of all, imagine that you could vanish from the face of the earth at any moment like a puff of smoke. Then you'll understand why I woke up that morning feeling pretty hopeless.

Gail and I got dressed and ate some hot Ralston in the kitchen, trying to fight away our gloomy moods. When we finished, Gail went into the living room to get Mom's diary. She wanted to read it one more time, I guess to convince herself that this was the past and that no matter what was happening now, everything would turn out all right in the end.

She came back into the kitchen looking as though she had seen a ghost.

"Chris," she said, holding the open diary in her hand, "it's empty."

I felt that funny hollow feeling creep inside me again. Only I knew it didn't have anything to do with disappearing this time; it was just plain dread.

"What do you mean, empty?"

"All the pages after December twenty-third. Chris. They're all blank. All of Mom's writing is gone."

I snatched the diary out of her hand and tore through the pages, all those pages we had read a hundred times up in our attic. It was true. Up to December twenty-third, 1955, everything was still there. But December twenty-fourth was a blank. Mom's description of how she'd run into Dad at Bradburn's was gone. As if her pen had never touched the page. And the rest of the diary was the same way—empty.

"That's not all," Gail added. "Look at the picture."

Her hand was shaking as she handed me the old photograph of Mom and Dad decorating his tree on Christmas Eve, 1955. I looked at Gail, and a thousand butterflies began frantically beating their wings against my insides.

"Look at it, Chris," she repeated, her voice dull and ominous.

I forced my eyes from Gail's face to the picture in my hand. It was blank, too.

———————CHAPTER FIFTEEN———————

———————CHAPTER FIFTEEN———————

Later that morning, in a daze, we headed for Christ the King. Gail and I had been doing more thinking than talking when she finally broke the silence.

"Chris? What does it mean, the diary and the picture going blank like that? I still don't get it."

"Well, I have an idea," I ventured. "It sort of reminds me of a Polaroid picture. After you take the picture, the blank film comes out of the camera. You know what you took a picture of; all you have to do is wait for it to develop itself. Only, in this case, no one took that picture of Mom and Dad last night. The picture was erased by our changing the past. It never happened. Now it's as though the picture is waiting to be taken. Only, it'll be a different picture—just what, I don't know."

"Or it could mean that the picture will stay blank forever."

"I don't think so. When you think about it, this is the first good sign we've had. If there wasn't going to be a picture of Mom and Dad, we wouldn't even have a blank. The picture just would have disappeared."

"Then the pages in the diary are waiting to be filled out, too. Only there will be new words. Something different."

"I think so. But who really knows?"

Gail shook her head and raised her face to the sky. "This whole thing's so confusing!"

"It's not nice to fool with Father Time," I joked. But the joke fell flat.

We arrived just in time for ten o'clock Christmas Mass. I should have known Mom and Dad would be there. They've never missed Mass in their lives. We spotted Mom in the crowded church sitting on the aisle halfway down, with our now younger Grandma and Grandpa Gilbert beside her. And there was Dad, sitting in the aisle seat directly across from her, with Aunt Alice and Grandma and Grandpa Davenport.

I wondered if this seating arrangement had been purely accidental or if one of them had spotted the other and maneuvered his or her family into sitting in the opposite pew. Gail and I hoped it was the latter.

We sat a few rows back so we could watch them. Throughout the Mass we saw Mom steal a glance at Dad, then Dad take a peek at Mom, in a game of hide-and-seek that lasted almost an hour. I have never seen so many phony excuses to turn sideways in all my life. Dad would cough and look at Mom. Then she would casually scan the pictures on the church walls and look at Dad. Then he would cast his gaze over the stained-glass windows and let it fall on her. Then she would yawn and turn toward him.

Gail and I watched all this silly business with increasing interest. Our hopes took giant leaps each time our parents' eyes secretly darted across the aisle to each other. All of this could only mean one thing: They were at least interested in each other. And I wondered if my push on the pond had started it.

But when the Mass was over, we followed our parents outside and watched in dismay as they got into their separate family cars and drove away without so much as another glance at each other.

Our spirits took a nose dive.

"Damn!"

"Chris!" Gail chided me. "Not in front of church on Christmas!"

"Well, I thought for sure *something* was going to happen. The way they were looking at each other. Good grief! I thought they would at least say *hello* to each other."

"So did I. I just can't understand it. I thought they were going to break the ice. And then, nothing." She looked down the street after both cars. "I just can't understand why they're acting that way. It makes me so mad!"

"Well, let's keep our appointment with Father Dooley. I don't know what he can do for us, but it has to be better than nothing."

We walked around to the rectory to wait for Father, while he wished everyone a merry Christmas on the front church steps. Ten minutes later we saw him heading our way.

"Good morning, Chris. Gail. Merry Chris—" He stopped himself and cleared his throat. "Well, come in, come in," he said, as he opened the door for us. "After you."

We all sat down, and for a couple of seconds no one said anything. Then the priest began seriously, "I thought over everything you two said yesterday, and if this is some kind of hoax, then you are the most convincing phonies I've ever run up against." He smiled at us with a strange twinkle in his deep blue eyes. "And now I'm going to ask you some questions about the future. I want the two of you to answer them as fast as you can. Do you understand? For the next several minutes, you are going to convince me that you are what you pretend to be—time travelers from the year 1983. Agreed?''

"Yes, Father," I replied, and swallowed. Gail simply nodded.

"Very well." He picked up a pencil and began writing on a pad. "Here's your first question."

And then we went through the most grueling oral exam of our lives. Father started by firing off questions about the names of people: the teachers we had had all through school, our principals, the store owners in town, our neighbors, all the way up to the names of the leaders of our government and foreign countries. Between the two of us, we managed to answer the questions as quickly as they were asked. Father Dooley jotted down all our replies. Then he went on to ask us broader questions: about wars, politics, social movements, inventions, natural disasters, music, radio, television, movies, clothing styles, cars, books, famous people, medicine, science, inflation, and all the problems the world was facing in 1983.

Finally, Father Dooley asked us about our parents, friends, and relatives. He wondered what kinds of changes the town had undergone in the last twenty-eight years, and what our lives were like in 1983. We kept batting the answers back as fast as Father Dooley threw them, even though some of it was a bit over our heads.

By the time we were finished, all three of us were thoroughly wiped out. We had gone on for over an hour.

"So," Father Dooley said at last, tapping his pencil on his note pad. He wore the face of a changed man. "So that's what the world is going to be like." His sharp blue eyes softened and had a far-off look in them.

"Then you do believe us?" I asked.

He rubbed his chin and nodded slowly. "I still don't know how you did it, but, yes, I do believe you. No one your age could invent so many answers so fast and make them all so convincing." Again, he aimed his eyes at my wrist. "And, of course, there's that watch of yours. I've made some inquiries, and no such watch exists. But, most of all, there's your knowledge of Father Ryan's coming. No one else knew. So there you have it."

Gail and I breathed a sigh of relief. We had passed the test.

"Do you realize," he said, "what you two have done? You've actually traveled through time. And not like H. G. Wells in a time machine, but simply by wishing yourselves back into the past. That's utterly incredible! But then," he added, almost to himself, "look at all the incredible things you've told me about: men walking on the moon, satellites circling the earth, nuclear-powered ships, heart and kidney transplants, computers the size of radios, and calculators the size of a watch. Simply amazing. Yet, all these things *are* possible. Anything is possible if you keep an open mind about it. Even, I suppose, being able to wish yourself into the past." He looked over at Gail and me with an expression that seemed an apology for his having doubted us. "Yes, I do believe you now, and I've got to help you."

"Oh, Father Dooley," Gail almost shouted. "If only you can."

"I can't promise anything, child. But I'll do everything that's within my power."

"Like what, Father?" I asked impatiently. "What *can* you do?"

"That, my boy, is a very good question. Somehow we have to get George Davenport and Elizabeth Gilbert to—how shall I say it? We have to get them together! We must help them to fall in love!" He had to smile at the ticklish situation he had been put in. "Good Lord. I've never had to play matchmaker before. I only hope I'm suited to the job."

He strolled back to his desk and sat down. "I've known these two children all their lives. I even baptized them. And I know their families. Good, honest people who attend church regularly." He glanced at Gail and shook his head. "I just can't believe that George and Elizabeth are your—" He straightened up. "Well, I'll do what I can now and think about all that later."

A minute went by when nobody said anything. Father Dooley sat in his chair, lost in thought. Then suddenly his face brightened up. "I have an idea. Yes! I think it might be just the thing!"

Gail and I sat up in our seats and asked together, "What?"

Father winked at us. "Listen—and pray that this works." He picked up his phone as he thumbed through the phone book, then dialed. "Hello, Mr. Davenport?" Father said cheerily into the receiver. "Father Dooley here. I hope you'll forgive this intrusion, but I forgot to ask your son to do me a favor when he was at Mass today. You know the church gives an annual Christmas dinner at the Peabody Home for the elderly. Well, I was going to ask George if he'd like to help out this afternoon by setting up the food, and maybe he'd even sing a few Christmas carols with the other youngsters. Your son's growing into a fine young man, and I think this would be a good opportunity for him to help people less fortunate than himself. It would be a good experience, don't you think? Yes, I'll hold on."

Father Dooley held the phone and winked at us again, smiling confidently. Then he spoke into the phone. "Oh, that's wonderful. Tell George how much I appreciate this. Tell him if he could come over to the school auditorium at one-thirty, we'll be ready to go by then. Fine. Thank you, Mr. Davenport. And merry Christmas."

Father Dooley hung up, wiping his brow. "So far, so good. Now one more call. Keep praying for me."

We did, while we held our breath.

He called Mom's house next and spoke directly to her. In just a few minutes it was all set. Mom was glad to join the group, too.

"There," the priest said after hanging up. He leaned back in his chair, looking rather proud of himself. "We are now on first base."

"Father," Gail exclaimed, "your idea is terrific!"

"It's more than that," I said. "It's pure genius."

"Now," Father said, "we must trust God to help us. Although," he added, "I'm not sure He's very pleased with what you two have done with His world."

Gail and I bowed our heads a little and lowered our eyes.

"But," Father Dooley quickly put in, "I'm sure He has forgiven you and understands that you couldn't ever have imagined what the consequences of your actions would be. So," he said as he stood up, "we have a great many things to do. Shall we get started?"

CHAPTER SIXTEEN

Ever since the church was built in the 1920s, it has been a tradition at Christ the King to provide a Christmas dinner for the Peabody Home, complete with donated turkeys and all the trimmings. And that's what Father Dooley was busy organizing now.

By a little after one in the afternoon, everyone began assembling in the auditorium. The boys in the church choir had trickled in one by one as their parents dropped them off, and were now practicing the carols they would sing at the home. Two girls and two boys, around my age, came into the large room. Father introduced them to Gail and me briefly. He understood that the less we talked to people, the less chance there was of our accidentally altering their futures. And he agreed to our coming only when we promised to stay away from Mom and Dad, and to try to avoid everyone else.

Gail and I pretended to be arranging the food that was piled in boxes on the stage. We kept to the far end of the auditorium with our backs to everyone. We kept glancing over our shoulders toward the door until we finally spotted Mom walk in. She was wearing a black skirt with a green turtleneck sweater that set off her long reddish hair and beautiful green eyes just fine. Father Dooley gave her a warm greeting and thanked her for coming. And just at that moment, Dad arrived.

Our young parents eyed each other with surprise.

We watched Father Dooley maintain his composure as he regarded our mother and father. But the look on his face, which he tried to conceal, said he still found it hard to believe that George and Liz were actually our parents.

"Elizabeth," Father Dooley said, "I think you know George Davenport, don't you?"

"We've met," Mom replied frostily.

But Father Dooley smiled all the more. "And George, you of course know Elizabeth Gilbert."

Dad cleared his throat a little. "Yeah. Hi, Liz."

Their eyes met, then dropped. They were completely embarrassed.

Mom turned away from Dad and focused on the priest. "How can I help, Father?"

Father Dooley's eyes bounced from Mom to Dad and back to Mom. "Why, how about if you and George start helping the others load everything into the cars? But first, I want you to say hello to the crew." Father Dooley led Mom and Dad over to the four other teenagers, whom they knew from the high school. Then Father went off to take care of some problem, leaving the six assistants alone.

"Gee, Sonny, what are you doing here?" Eddy Driscol asked. He was the kind of guy who asked a lot of questions. "Are you really going to help us out? When did you start getting involved in church stuff?"

Then Linda Drysler—dark haired, beautiful, and sultry—slid up to Dad and cooed, "This is a nice surprise, Sonny. Looks like our little party is going to be more fun than I expected."

A guy named Sid Beauchamp tried to act cool

111

around Dad. "How ya doin', man," he drawled. "Looks like you and me are gonna have to make the best outta this gig, eh? Just think what the gang would say if they saw us here playin' Santa Claus. I mean, wow."

Bonny Sutton, who was short, loud, and spoke her mind, retorted, "Get off it, Sid. This is probably the biggest thing you've done since you fell off your back porch."

Sid ignored her and asked my dad, "How'd *you* get rooked into doin' this, Sonny?"

The four of them looked at Dad.

"Oh," Dad replied casually, "Father Dooley asked me to. I didn't have anything better to do. You know."

Linda Drysler edged closer to Dad and used her best husky voice on him. "Where's your girl friend Becky? I can't imagine you being *anywhere* without dear little Becky."

Dad smiled humorlessly. "I don't know where she is. And I don't care."

"Well," Linda said, "did you two lovebirds have an argument?" Then she turned her big brown eyes up at Dad. "Or did Becky finally let you off her chain?"

"Back off, Linda," Bonny warned. "Your fangs are showing."

It seemed like it took a full minute for Linda's eyes to swing over to Bonny. "Bonny," she sang, "why don't you take a flying leap off a very high bridge?" With that, she nestled closer to Dad, batting her eyelashes at him. "Whenever you get tired of Becky, well, you know my number."

Bonny couldn't resist that. "Oh, Sonny's got your number, all right. Don't worry about that, Linda-poo."

Sid let out a horselaugh over that, and, because he did, Eddy Driscol did, too.

While this conversation was taking place, Mom was edging off to the side. Her face grew dark and her eyes threw daggers at Linda Drysler. She was steaming!

"I saw you blow Wild Bill's bird off the road, Sonny," Sid said. "Boy, was that ever cool. I knew he couldn't take you. You've got the hottest machine around."

"He's right," Linda cooed at Dad. "You *are* the hottest guy around."

"No, Linda-going-deaf-poo," Bonny smirked. "The word was machine. Machine!"

"And I bet you could take Art Johnson's Chevy if you wanted, huh?" Sid added. "Your car could eat his Chevy for breakfast."

Pint-sized Eddy Driscol piped up, "Who's Art Johnson?"

Bonny had to shake her head. "Never mind, Eddy. Just go back to sleep."

Curiously enough, Dad didn't seem too interested in talking about cars. He kept glancing at Mom.

"Could you take him?" Eddy asked my dad. "Could you?"

"Oh, I guess I could," he answered Eddy, with only a pinch of conceit in his voice. "If I wanted to."

And just then, almost out of nowhere, after being totally forgotten by the others, Mom took a step forward. She looked straight at Dad and asked, "Why would you?"

Everyone was taken aback. They stared at her as though they hadn't understood her question.

"Why?" she repeated boldly.

Dad blinked at her, and I could see the first traces of pink spreading over his face. "Why, what?"

"Why do you need to drag this Art Johnson? Why do you need to drag *anyone*?"

"Why?" Dad repeated, his voice sounding unsure. "You mean, why drag?"

"I believe that's still the question."

Everyone looked thunderstruck, as though they had never heard such a question before.

"Because . . ." Dad began.

"Yes?" Mom leveled her lovely but piercing green eyes at him.

Dad seemed hypnotized. "Because it's . . . it's . . ."

"Yes. Go on."

Everyone's mouth hung half open, all eyes going from the flustered boy to the demanding girl.

"Because," Dad managed to sputter, "it's a sport."

All mouths shut in unison, spreading into satisfied smirks.

"Yeah," Bonny said. "So why do you care, Liz?"

"Oh," Mom said casually, "I just wanted to know why anyone would want to break the law and risk his neck just for some stupid sport. It seems rather silly, doesn't it?"

"Oh, brother," Bonny groaned, with upturned eyes. "Are you ever square."

"Yeah. Get with it, Liz," Sid said, for everyone's benefit.

"Oh, Liz," Linda said, "you live such a sheltered life. You never have gotten out of the bicycle stage, have you?"

"Yeah," Bonny sneered. "I bet she's never been in a hot rod in her life."

I saw Mom get that look in her eye I knew so well. I could recognize it, although she was only sixteen. Even then, it spelled big trouble. And she was just about to let them all have it when Father Dooley—who must have overheard what was going on—rushed up to save the day. "All right, everyone," he said, trying to divert their attention. "It's time for us to go. The choir's leaving now. Why don't we all gather up the food and follow them? Ready, everyone? That's it. That's it."

Father Dooley gently herded the six teenagers into action while Gail and I scrambled off to the far side of the stage, away from everyone. The kids picked up the boxes and grocery bags of food and started making their way out the door. That was when Father Dooley gave Gail and me the signal to follow. The plan was for us to get into Father Dooley's car and tag along with him. But we were still to keep out of everyone's way as much as possible—especially our parents'. Also, Father was to organize the car pooling in such a way that Mom would ride along with Dad in his hot rod, while the four others went in Sid Beauchamp's old Studebaker.

Well, that was the way it was supposed to happen. As usual, things went wrong.

"Elizabeth," Father Dooley said to my mother, as everyone walked out into the freezing air, "I'm afraid my car and Sid's car are going to be rather full. Why don't you ride along with George?"

Dad, who had opened the door of Father Dooley's car and unloaded the box he was carrying onto the back seat, said, "I don't think Liz wants to ride with me, Father." Then he looked at Mom. "Do you?"

Mom got that prim look on her face and said to Father Dooley, "I'll ride with him if he promises not to drag anybody on the way there."

Well, you should have seen my Dad's face. I thought he was going to blow up right there on the spot. Instead, he managed to control himself and say to Father Dooley, "You can tell Liz for me that she doesn't have anything to worry about."

"Good," Mom answered Dad directly, her chin an inch higher in the air. "Then I'll take a chance."

That over, Father Dooley got behind the wheel of his '39 Dodge, hit the starter, and listened in dismay as it groaned to a quick death. Dad walked over to the front of the car, popped the hood, and fooled around a bit while Father Dooley hit the starter again. But the car was deader than a doornail.

"Sorry, Father," Dad said, slamming down the hood. "Look's like your battery's shot." He smiled, adding, "Only a miracle can save *this* car."

Father tried to smile but couldn't. No one except my sister and Father Dooley and I realized the terrible problem this was about to create.

Sid and the others came over. "Come on, Father," Sid said. "You can come with us." With that, everyone started transferring the food in the Dodge over to Sid's Studebaker. "There's enough room for us," he said. "Linda can sit on Bonny's lap."

Bonny yelled, "Real funny, Sidney! How about if we paint you silver and let you go as the hood ornament!"

And before Father Dooley could do or say anything, Dad looked over at Gail and me standing stranded by the dead Dodge and said to us, "You two can ride with us. There's room in the rumble seat."

Gail and I had already thrown our mufflers over our mouths to conceal our faces. Apparently Dad didn't recognize Gail from the other day when she ran into him at the store. So far, so good. But now look what was happening! We were being forced into riding with our mom and dad, when we were supposed to stay away from them!

Things happened so fast that we lost control of the situation. Father Dooley gave me a distressed glance and headed for Sid's car. He called back over his shoulder, "It's got to be this way, Chris. Go with them. I'll see you later."

"Here," Dad said to Gail and me, as the four of us walked up to his red hot rod. "Just climb into the rumble seat back there. Keep your faces covered, and it won't be so bad." For Mom's benefit he added, "And I promise I'll drive slowly so you won't freeze to death." Then he said to Mom, "And I'll even put my top up for you."

"Oh, don't do that," Mom said, mocking Linda. "How will I *ever* get out of my bicycle stage if I don't ride in a hot rod with the top down?" She batted her eyelashes.

My sister and I climbed into the rumble seat, scared out of our skulls, wondering how in the world we were going to survive this mess.

Mom looked back at us as she opened the door on her side and asked, "Have you ever ridden in a hot rod with the top down?"

Gail answered from behind her muffler, "I think we're all about to come out of our bicycle stages."

And with that, the girls winked at each other and smiled.

Dad ignored Mom's little performance and fired up his engine. A blast of noise rolled out of both tailpipes. I saw Mom shoot Dad a warning glance. Dad saw it, eased up on the gas pedal, put the car in gear, and slowly let out the clutch.

Gail and I mentally crossed our fingers, and the next thing I knew, we were off!

CHAPTER SEVENTEEN

I wonder if you have any idea how weird it was for us to be riding in the rumble seat of a hot rod in winter with our teenage parents up front. I mean, it was downright crazy!

So there Gail and I were, scrunched down in this tight space that was nothing more than a double seat sunk in the trunk, going down the street with the upper part of our bodies sticking out in the cold wind, mufflers over our faces, our eyes wide and staring in disbelief, looking like complete idiots.

With the top down, my sister and I had no trouble overhearing everything that was being said up front.

"I want to apologize again for running into you on the pond," Dad said to Mom. "I sure hope I didn't break anything."

"That's all right," Mom replied coolly. "Us Gilberts can take anything you Davenports can dish out."

Dad jerked his head toward Mom, who was staring straight ahead. "Now what in the heck is *that* supposed to mean?"

"Nothing," she answered in that same frigid, holier-than-thou tone she sometimes uses with Gail and me when she wants to drive a point home.

"Look," Dad said heatedly, "I'm just trying to be . . . Ah, the heck with it." His eyes went back to the road. "Why did you come with me, anyway? I'm sure you would have enjoyed yourself a lot more with the others."

"Maybe."

"So? Why did you decide to ride with me?"

"Because I've always wanted to get into this *thing* you call a car. Just think. Now I can tell everyone that I actually rode in the great Sonny Davenport hot rod. Wow, gee whiz, and neato."

"Oh, is that so? No one else has ever complained—"

"You don't have to get angry. It isn't my fault that you can't own a normal car."

"And what's wrong with this car, I'd like to know?"

"It looks like the car of somebody who wants to prove something to the world. *Are* you trying to prove something to the world?"

"Are you kidding? I'm not trying to prove anything!"

"Then why do you look and act like you are?"

"What's that supposed to mean?"

Mom looked at Dad for the first time. "Only that you act like you need to have everyone in town gawking at you. But what you've done is get everyone to notice your *car*. Without it, you're—" But Mom didn't finish the sentence. "Maybe you need to start giving more thought to yourself, and a little less to this contraption of yours."

Dad gave Mom a fierce look, then turned back to the road with a frown. From my angle in the rumble seat I could see he was doing more thinking than driving. Then Dad said, "At least I own my own car. Not like some rich guys who drive their mommies' new white Oldsmobiles."

Now it was Mom's turn to get mad. "Johnny's saving *his* money for college. At least *he's* going to make something out of himself."

"Oh, yeah? And what's *that* supposed to mean?"

"It means there are more important things to do with your life than spend it on a car. Things like growing up."

Dad pulled up to the corner stop sign and gave his passenger a bitter, hurt look. "So. We're on that one again, eh? You're beginning to sound a lot like my parents, you know that? They always preach at me, too."

"Maybe you should start listening to them."

Dad threw his gearshift into first and roared away from a standing stop, nearly snapping all our heads off.

"You don't have to show off for me," Mom said casually. "If you can't drive right, then you can just let me out and I'll walk."

Dad shot another angry look at Mom and opened his mouth to say something, but Mom beat him to it. "Besides, I'm not like Becky Steel. I don't need those kinds of thrills. Really."

The words just flew out of Dad's mouth. "No! You're not anything like Becky or anybody else! You're the Brain! You and Bennett, two of a kind! You both think you're so far above us average people! Always looking down on us!" Dad clenched his jaw and gripped the steering wheel hard.

Mom stiffened in her seat. "I don't look down on anybody!"

"Oh, yes you do," Dad growled, shaking his head, grinning bitterly. He kept his eyes straight ahead. "*Everybody* knows you do."

Mom's frown darkened. "Your problem is that you just don't want to act like an adult. You see people take life seriously and you think they're square. But let them go hot rodding around like morons and you think they're cool. That's the way *you* look at the world!''

"Oh, yeah? And your problem is that you don't know how to enjoy life. All you want to do is impress everyone with how smart you are.''

"Very funny. You're a real riot." But Mom couldn't hide the hurt in her voice.

"The Brain," Dad mumbled.

"Stop calling me that!''

"Sorry," he said, but didn't sound like he meant it.

Gail and I couldn't believe what we were hearing. If you knew how friendly and caring and loving our parents are, then you'd understand why we were so flabbergasted by the way they were acting—like a couple of dumb kids. But, once again, we had to remind ourselves that that's just what they were—kids.

Just where all this bickering was leading to had me worried. Gail, too. Then I began to realize that something important was going on between them. As adults, I've heard my parents say things to each other, when all the time they really meant something else. You had to read between the lines, and that's what we were trying to do. In a way, they were giving each other messages—testing each other.

They were still going at it up front—and by now Dad wasn't paying any attention to his driving—when all of a sudden he ran a stop sign. I'd wanted to yell out a warning but the less he noticed me, the better. All I could do was hold my breath as we went zipping through the intersection. And, wouldn't you know it? There was a cop coming toward us from the other street who saw the whole thing. And before Dad knew what had happened, a black 1952 Ford with large white letters spelling POLICE pulled us over.

Gail and I were on the verge of heart attacks when the policeman strolled toward us. We were trapped inside the rumble seat. I wondered what would happen if he wanted to take us all in. What were we going to say? That we lived at 544 Chestnut Street, when somebody else owned the house? And can you imagine his asking where our parents were? If we answered that one, they'd put Gail and me in the nut factory for sure.

We hitched our mufflers a little higher over our cold noses, gritted our teeth, and hoped for the best.

The cop stepped up to Dad's side of the car. "You know you ran that stop sign back there, don't you?"

"Yes, sir," Dad replied. "I guess I didn't see it. I'm sorry."

"You're Sonny Davenport, aren't you?"

"Yes, sir."

The cop stood back a little, admiring Dad's car. "You know, when I was a little younger, I always wanted to have a car like this." Then he straightened up and said in an authoritative tone, "Okay, let me see your driver's license."

Dad handed it over to him, and the cop checked it over. As he took out his summons pad, he looked at Gail and me in the rumble seat. "Little cold back there, isn't it, kids?"

"You can say that again, officer," I replied as casually as I could.

The cop turned back to Dad. "Didn't you see that stop sign coming up? I sure do hate to give anybody a ticket on Christmas. I was hoping to go the whole day without any trouble, and now you've gone and ruined everything." He actually grinned at Dad. "Got any good excuses? I'm willing to listen."

Then Mom—who had been hiding behind her coat collar—sat up, grinning at the cop. "He's got the best excuse in the world, Uncle Ted. I was giving him a razz."

The cop—Uncle Ted—looked past Dad. "Liz! What in the world are you—" He gave a quick glance back at Dad, then said to her, "Now, what's all this about a razz? And it better be good."

He walked over to the other side of the car, and the next thing we knew, Mom was having a friendly chat with her uncle Ted (who turned out to be the great-uncle Ted I'd heard Mom talk about—a retired police officer now living in Florida). Mom informed Uncle Ted that we were on our way to the Peabody Home to help out with the Christmas dinner, that she had been giving Dad a hard time, and that she was the cause of his running the stop sign. The result was that Uncle Ted gave Dad a warning about driving more carefully, handed back his driver's license, and wished us all a merry Christmas.

Dad thanked the policeman, put his car in gear, and drove quietly away as we all breathed a sigh of relief.

Dad looked at Mom with a changed expression on his face. "Liz, you saved my neck. Thanks."

A tiny smile played on her lips as Mom gazed straight ahead out the windshield. "Oh, you don't have to thank me, George. It was a pleasure."

Dad did a double take when she called him by his real name. He grinned back. "You're really something, you know that . . . Elizabeth."

She turned toward him and answered playfully, "I know. So are you."

That was it. I could feel it. There are such things as turning points in a person's life, and I was sure this was one of them. There's also such a thing as chemistry between two people, and I could almost hear the bubbling and fizzing in the front seat.

Gail elbowed me excitedly with a smile in her eyes, and I signaled back with the old thumbs up. And the four of us continued chugging merrily down the street.

CHAPTER EIGHTEEN

Gail and I were ready to jump out of Dad's rumble seat the instant he parked his car in front of the Peabody Home. Father Dooley, who was looking pretty panicky because we had taken so long, hurried over as we pulled up to the curb.

"Hurry up, hurry up," he said to Gail and me. "There are things to do, and you're late as it is. That's it, hurry." We lost no time getting out of there, while Father Dooley did a good job of keeping Mom and Dad busy and away from us.

Gail and I were put in charge of the kitchen. We made ourselves useful by heating up the turkeys and sweet potatoes and corn. Father Dooley's other assistants gathered in the living room to listen to the boys' choir sing carols.

I opened the swinging kitchen door a little and poked my head out. The spacious living room was decorated with a huge Christmas tree and ropes of holly, and the sound of Christmas was everywhere. The room was filled with music and the spicy smell of cinnamon cider. All the old folks sat around the singers in chairs, some in wheelchairs. There must have been about forty of them. Some nodded along with the music, while others joined in the singing. This was the time of the year they most looked forward to, when

Christ the King and Father Dooley brought Christmas cheer into their lives.

I could see Linda and Bonny, Sid and Eddy standing against the wall in the living room, looking pretty pleased at the happiness they had brought. Mom was by the fireplace, singing aloud in the same high vibrato voice that sang nursery rhymes when I was little. Dad added his full, deep voice. They were smiling at each other as they joined the choir in "Hark! the Herald Angels Sing."

I closed the kitchen door and reported what I'd seen to Gail.

"They're smiling at each other?" She ran over to the door and peeked out for herself. After a long moment, she said, "It's going to be all right now, isn't it, Chris? You can see it in their faces. They *do* like each other." She let out a heavy sigh. "We'll be able to go back home soon, won't we?"

"I sure hope so," I replied, as we both looked through the doorway again. "If anything else goes wrong, I don't think I'll be able to take it."

And sure enough, something went wrong.

Just then, Gail cried out, "Oh, no!" Because who should come waltzing through the front door but Becky Steel! "What's *she* doing here?"

"I don't know," I said, banging my fist against the kitchen door. "She must have found out Dad is here and now she's going to throw a wrench into the whole works!" I started going through the doorway. "You stay here while I check things out."

"But Father Dooley told us to stay in the kitchen."

"He didn't say that exactly. He just told us not to talk to anyone unless absolutely necessary. And I'm not going to. Don't worry."

I made my way through the crowd to the back of the

living room. I hid not far from Mom and Dad, just in time to see Becky walk up to Father Dooley, who was standing beside Dad.

"Hello, Father," Becky greeted him in an obviously controlled voice. Her anger at seeing Dad there with Mom was written all over her face. "I think my mother forgot to bring her pie over to the church this year, so I brought this one over for her."

"But," Father replied, "she did bring one over. This morning, in fact."

"Oh, really?" Becky said innocently. "Oh, well. Then here's an extra one. I'm sure it won't go to waste."

"Why, thank you, Becky, That's very generous of you. Why don't you take it into the kitchen. I have some helpers in there who will take care of it for you."

There was one helper in there who would like to take care of Becky's pie, all right.

Then Becky acted as though she had just noticed Dad for the first time. "Oh, hi, Sonny. I didn't know you were here."

Dad's demeanor had changed when he spotted Becky. He attempted a cordial smile, but I could see he was really ticked off at her for coming. "Father Dooley asked me to help out," he said curtly.

Becky had to have heard the irritation in his voice. She shrugged it off, gathered herself, and turned to Mom. "Well, if it isn't Liz Gilbert. Fancy seeing you here."

"Hello, Becky," Mom answered in her best wintry tones. "Father Dooley asked me to help out, too."

"Well," Becky replied, her eyes darting from Mom to Dad. "Aren't we busy little elves today?" Then, to Father Dooley, "Can I help out, too, Father? As long as I'm here, I may as well do something useful."

Just then the choir finished singing "Joy to the World," and the living room was filled with applause.

"Help out?" the old priest said. "Why, thank you, Becky. That's very kind of you. I'd appreciate it if you helped serve, if you wouldn't mind. We can always use an extra pair of hands."

"Mind?" she said, averting her eyes from Mom's icy stare. "No. Of course not. I'd be glad to."

It was plain that Becky was out to make trouble for Dad. She had that look in her eye. And poor Father Dooley had fallen right into her trap. But then, how was he to know that Becky was dating Dad? We had never thought to tell him.

I went back to the kitchen and quickly told Gail the bad news. She hit the roof just as Becky came walking in with her pie. "Where do you want me to put this?" Becky asked.

"You *really* want to know!" Gail said.

I quickly said, "You can put it over there with the others."

She did, then retorted on her way out, "Real friendly people around here!" The swinging door went *thump-thump* behind her.

Gail folded her arms and scowled at the kitchen door. "Now what do we do with *her* in the way?"

"What *can* we do? Nothing. We just sit tight and see what happens."

Just then, Father Dooley stuck his head in. "Time to set up dinner."

I told Father Dooley about the problem we were going to have with Becky around, but we all reluctantly agreed that it was too late to do anything about it. Father sighed, then left us.

Gail and I handed out the food we'd warmed up to Mom, Dad, and the others, who took it out. Card tables had been set up in the living room and the adjacent music room, as well as in the large glassed-in sunroom that ran the full length of the west side of the house. Since only twelve residents could fit at the dining room table at a time, eating at card tables was probably part of their daily routine.

The kids weren't eating because they would have Christmas dinner in their own homes afterward. But Gail and I intended to fill up on as much turkey and trimmings as we could. After all, we didn't have any dinner or home to go to.

Father Dooley did his best to seat our key players in the most advantageous spots but, as usual, things didn't work out as planned. After Mom and Dad had finished putting out the food, they strolled together into the sunroom to sit at the card table Father had reserved for them. Meanwhile, Father Dooley asked Becky to carry some extra bowls of vegetables into the dining room so she wouldn't see where Mom and Dad had disappeared to. Then, thinking his mission had been accomplished, Father Dooley joined our parents at their table. But no sooner had he sat down than Becky ran up and plopped into the fourth chair. Father Dooley looked confused, Dad scowled, and Mom gave Becky a glare that should have given her first-degree frostbite.

In a way, I felt sorry for Becky. She was obviously putting on a brave front, and she wore the expression of a soldier going into battle knowing he was low on ammunition. But my pity for her didn't last long. I wanted her away from my parents—now! I even contemplated walking up behind her and accidentally spilling something on her in the hope that she would have to go home to clean up, but I couldn't bring myself to do something as gauche as that. I didn't mention this idea to Gail. Something told me that if I did, Becky would end up wearing three pounds of hot creamed peas.

Gail and I quickly sat ourselves at a table near our parents. Two old ladies joined us and proceeded to talk our ears off. It wasn't easy, but I did manage to hear everything that was said nearby.

"George," Father Dooley said, "it could be my imagination, but I don't think we've exchanged more than ten words this year." He winked playfully. "Now why is that, I wonder?"

"I suppose that's my fault, Father," Dad replied. "I guess when Mass is over, I'm the first one out the door."

Father Dooley chuckled. "Don't feel too guilty about that. I did the same thing when I was young. It seemed like there was always so much to do, and I couldn't wait to do it."

Father Dooley was obviously trying to make conversation, but wasn't quite sure how to do it. He turned to Mom next. "Elizabeth, I've been hearing some good things about your grades in school. Do you still plan to do something with your piano?"

"Yes, Father," Mom replied. "I want to teach piano and music some day."

"And where do you intend to study after high school?"

"I thought I'd go to the University of Missouri."

"Good. That's a fine school. Who knows, you just might come back to Summerville and teach music at the high school."

"I'm not sure what I'll do. But you never can tell."

Then the old priest went back to Dad. "George, your time in school is coming to a close. What are your plans after graduation? Any ideas yet?"

To everyone's shock—mine especially—Becky Steel blurted, "I guess you haven't heard, Father. The only plan Sonny has is to stay in school for another year."

Dad looked completely mortified. He blushed and confessed, "I—I won't be graduating this year." Then he shot a dagger look at Becky and lowered his eyes.

"But why?" Father Dooley asked, surprised.

Dad cleared his throat. "I . . . guess there are some classes I need to take over."

"I *guess*!" Becky said with savage delight. "He flunked four of them!" She looked defiantly at Mom and Dad, pleased with the trouble she had caused.

But Mom rose to the occasion. "Why, Becky," she said, "it was very kind of you to inform us about the problems George is having in school. Is there anything else you think we should know?"

Becky blinked across the table at Mom. It was written all over her face that she knew she had made a disastrous mistake.

But before Becky could say anything to remedy her blunder, Mom added, "I guess that means George will be with us another year, while you go off to college, isn't that right, Becky?" And, not waiting for an answer, she turned to Dad and smiled. "Looks like you and I will just have to hold down the fort while Becky's gone. Right, George?"

Dad looked at Mom as though he couldn't believe what he was hearing. His tense face eased into a smile. "I guess we will, Liz."

Their eyes locked, their smiles fading into something serious.

"How did it happen, George?" Mom asked. "Your grades, I mean."

Becky, who was almost trembling with rage, snapped at Mom. "His name's Sonny!"

But Mom ignored her.

Dad did, too. He shook his head, then shrugged. "What can I say? It's not that I couldn't have made good grades. It's just that . . . I guess I really wasn't trying. I skipped some classes—too many, actually— to work on my car, and—" He gave Mom a quick glance at the mention of his hot rod, but her accepting smile didn't change. Dad continued, "I guess I really blew it. All because of that stupid car!"

Mom's eyebrows arched at the unexpected statement.

Becky looked at Dad like he was a complete stranger. "I don't believe what you just said. What's gotten into you all of a sudden? Calling your car stupid."

"You're right." He glared at her. "It's not my car that's stupid. It's me!"

"I don't get this." Becky frowned. "You've never acted like this before. What's going on with you?"

"Is it so hard to figure out? You want me to paint you a picture? All right, I will. You and all the seniors will be going off to college or getting jobs or going into the armed forces, or something. You'll all be going ahead in life, and I'll be left behind. Me!" He emphasized by jabbing his thumb at himself. "Me! Left behind! I've been an idiot! I've been so busy having a good time—and now I realize that I've been *wasting* my time. And it's a little late, but I'm beginning to realize that none of my friends really cared!"

"Well, don't blame *me*," Becky nearly yelled. "*I*

132

didn't make you waste your time. You did that all by yourself."

Good old Mom came to the rescue again. She picked up where she had left off as though nothing had happened. "Which classes are you having trouble with, George?"

Dad regained his composure. "Well, the toughest is algebra. I just know I'm going to flunk my finals in it."

"Algebra?" Mom displayed her perfect teeth. "I love algebra. I could help you with that."

"You could?" Dad suddenly perked up. "You—you'd be willing to help me?"

"Sure. Why not?"

"I think that's a fine idea," Father Dooley quickly broke in. "Don't you think so, George?"

Dad looked at the old gentleman, then at Mom. "But why? Why would you want to help me?"

"Because," Mom answered simply, "maybe it's about time somebody started helping you, instead of only *using* you."

Becky Steel, who was smoldering on the other side of the table, suddenly burst out, "I could help you, too, you know! All you have to do is ask me!"

Dad looked at her as if seeing her for the first time. "But you never offered to help me before. Not once. Why are you doing it now?"

Becky opened her mouth to answer, but nothing came out.

Dad turned back to Mom. "Thanks, Liz. That would be a nice Christmas present. When would you like to—"

"Start? Anytime. Whenever you want to, George."

Becky finally boiled over. "What's all this *George* stuff, anyway? What's going on around here?" She turned her blazing eyes on Dad. "I thought we were going steady. What's happening with you?"

Mom ignored Becky. She said to Dad, "How about after we leave here, if that's okay with you? Since you're driving me home anyway, I could stop by your house and take a look at your math book."

Dad sat up two inches in his chair. "Today?"

"Sure." She gave him her warmest smile. "Why not?"

Becky jumped right out of her chair, knocking it over. "So that's the way it is, is it? Sonny Davenport, don't ever speak to me again!" And with that, she stormed out of the room. But not out of the Home, I observed. She hesitated in the front hall, then slumped into a chair there, looking as wounded and miserable as she could, knowing Dad could see her from where he sat.

But Dad wasn't buying Becky's theatrics. "Don't worry about her," he said, more for Father Dooley's benefit than for Mom's. "She'll survive."

I could see by Father Dooley's expression that he knew it was time to make himself scarce. He excused himself and left.

Mom looked at Dad seriously. "Would it be an understatement to say that Becky's mad?"

Dad shrugged. "She thinks she owns me."

"Well, aren't you two going steady?"

"No. Not that I know of."

"But you're with her all the time. Or so it seems."

"Yeah, well, I'm not chained to her. Know what I mean?"

Their eyes met and held for a moment.

"Sure. I know."

Dad shifted around in his chair, suddenly appearing agitated. "Look, Liz, you don't have to help me with my math if you don't want to. The mistakes I made in school are my own stupid fault, and I'm the one who has to correct them." He glanced at her, then looked at the tablecloth. "You're way too smart to concern yourself with bailing out somebody like me. I mean, you're a super student. You've got it made. You know where you're going. You've got better things to do than mop up after my spills. I really appreciate the offer, but now that I think about it—"

"George," Mom cut in. "I *want* to help you. Don't you believe me?"

"Yeah," he managed to answer. "I believe you. But . . ."

"But what?"

"What I still don't understand is . . . why?"

Mom's face started turning pink. "Because I like you," she said, forcing herself not to look down.

"You do?" Dad stared at her incredulously.

And would you believe it? Just at that critical moment, the woman in charge of the Peabody Home rushed over to Mom with outstretched arms. "Elizabeth Gilbert! I thought that was you over here. Remember me? Melissa Cole? I met you last summer at your mother's. You were practicing your piano, and you played some Chopin for us that was *simply* delightful. I thought I might ask you to play something for us now, if you wouldn't mind. Everyone would be so grateful if you did."

Mom, caught by surprise, of course consented and found herself being led away by the kindly old lady. Mom glanced back at Dad, shrugged, smiled, and disappeared into the music room.

Dad looked angry at Mom's being whisked away. But I felt something else was bothering him, too. Something more important than that. He looked at

Becky still sulking in the front hall, then at the music room, then down at his hands, deep in thought.

Well, Dad had said the one thing Gail and I wanted to hear—that he wanted to change. And Mom had admitted that she liked him. That definitely put us on second base, even though my parents didn't know it at the moment. Things were looking up.

Gail and I excused ourselves from our two old ladies and made our way into the back of the music room, out of everyone's way. We listened to Mom's interpretation of Chopin's "Minute Waltz," and when she finished, we proudly joined in the applause. Then, when her audience insisted on an encore, she began to play Chopin's E-flat Nocturne.

I took my eyes off her just in time to see something I couldn't believe. Dad had his jacket on and was walking out the front door, with Becky following right behind him! I nudged Gail and jerked my head toward the door. "Stop him!" she whispered loudly, and jumped out of her chair. But Father Dooley—who had seen everything—rushed up and took Gail by the arm, shaking his head vigorously. Then he led us into the kitchen, out of earshot.

"Don't do it, Gail," he said. "You can't interfere with the past any more, no matter what happens. It's too dangerous. Haven't you learned that lesson by now?"

Gail wasn't in any mood to listen. "But we can't let it fall apart now! Not when we're this close! We've got to do *something*, Father!"

I said to Father Dooley, "I thought everything was going all right. From what I could hear, Mom and Dad were hitting it off just fine. What happened? I don't get it."

The priest shook his head. "I don't know what happened, either. Unless . . ."

"Unless what?" Gail wanted to know.

"Well," he said, sitting down on a kitchen chair, "look at it this way. I think we can all agree that your parents are attracted to each other. Am I right?"

"But," Gail interrupted, "Dad took off with Mrs. McConnell! Why would he do that?"

Father Dooley smiled. "I think your father is going through a change. He's reached a crossroads in his life. A time of decision. And it could be that he doesn't know how to handle it. He may be afraid."

"Afraid?" Gail repeated.

"Yes, afraid. George is maturing quickly. Maybe faster than he knows how to cope with. Your mother made an offer to help him, and I think he's not sure how to deal with it. It could be that he's running away from the situation."

"But Dad wouldn't run away from any situation," Gail insisted. "He's not like that."

"That," Father reminded her, "is the adult George you're talking about."

Gail looked stubbornly at both of us. "He'll come back," she said.

"Well," Father Dooley sighed, "I certainly hope so. Because I don't know what more we can do. It's out of our hands. Now let's go out there and listen to your mother play."

The three of us went back to the music room and stood against the far wall. Mom was just finishing her piece. Again, the room filled with applause. Smiling, she turned and bowed to her admirers. But her smile faded as she scanned the room for Dad. Then she looked out into the foyer and saw that Becky was missing, too. Her complexion turned pale. She ran

137

between the card tables to the sunroom and saw that Dad wasn't there, either. Then she darted to a window and looked out onto the street. What she saw was written all over her face: Dad's car was gone.

Father Dooley had started walking toward Mom when Mrs. Cole rushed up to her. " My dear, you played beautifully! Marvelously! Could we get you to play just once more? Please?"

Mom turned around. Mrs. Cole gasped. "Why, you're cry—"

But Mom ignored the old woman and marched past her to the music room, her fists clenched. The old people spotted her heading back for the piano and began to clap.

"What's Mom going to do?" Gail asked, as we followed her to the music room.

"Can't you guess?"

"You mean—"

"Why not? Like adult, like teenager."

In other words, our mother was about to have one of her cathartic bouts at the piano. As far back as I can remember, Mom's always expressed her moods at the piano. When she's blue, she plays the blues. When she's happy, she plays something light and bouncy. Thoughtful, something slow and meditative. And when she's angry, she can pound out something that resembles a Missouri thunderstorm. I could see by her expression that we were all in for a real drencher.

Mom sat down at the piano amid the applause and glared at the keyboard. When her fingers struck the keys, it sounded like the skies had suddenly burst open. Again and again she hit the keys, sounding a fury of dissonant chords that made everyone sit up and blink in astonishment.

"Oh, my!" a gray-haired woman beside me exclaimed. "What *is* that girl *doing*?"

An elderly man sitting beside her shook his head. "She sure sounds riled up about something, don't she?"

Table after table of old people put down their knives and forks and stared bemused at the girl venting her emotion on their piano. The music (if it could be called that) reverberated off the walls, almost making the overhead chandelier swing. And just as it reached a stormy crescendo, I saw the front door open.

And in walked Dad.

CHAPTER NINETEEN

I nudged Gail and nodded toward the closing front door. Her face lit up like a Christmas tree, and tears of relief and joy sprang to her eyes.

"Dad," she whispered. "Oh, Dad, you came back. I knew you would."

We watched him walk through the front hall into the music room. His eyes never left Mom, who continued filling the house with thunder. It was as though he knew what she was doing, could almost understand what she was saying through the music.

Then Dad walked through the maze of seated people up to the piano and stood next to Mom. She turned her head sideways and looked up into his face.

The last resounding chord hung in the air between them and faded into nothing. For one long moment the entire world fell silent.

The two young people stared into each other's eyes . . . and smiled.

Mom suddenly realized that everyone was looking at them. A bewildered mumbling swept the room. Then, like a real trouper, she turned back to the piano and began playing an entirely different piece. And what she played was something gentle and beautiful and full of love. A budding love for my father, I could tell.

The music worked its magic on everyone. All the old people relaxed and settled back in their chairs, and when Mom finished, they gave her a big ovation. She stood before her admirers, bowing slightly. Pride was written all over Dad's face.

A few minutes later, it was time for all of us to leave. Father Dooley rounded everyone up for one last song, "We Wish You a Merry Christmas," which Gail and I sang from the back of the room in our loudest and best voices. When we finished singing, the woman in charge of the home stood up and gave us a little speech, thanking us for everything we had done.

The next thing I knew, I saw Mom and Dad heading for the front door with their coats on. Gail and I made our way through the crowded room while our parents disappeared. We rushed to the window just in time to see them get into my grandfather's 1953 De Soto.

"So that's why Dad left," Gail said, as we watched them pull away. "He didn't want to take Mom home in his hot rod."

"Then what happened to Becky?"

"She probably just followed him out. Maybe he took her home. Who knows? Who cares? The important thing is that Dad's finally with the right girl."

Then a familiar voice came from behind us. Father Dooley put his warm hands on our shoulders. "We did it," he said. "Thank God, everything worked out for the best."

"Amen," we both said.

Rather than hitch a ride with someone, Father Dooley, Gail, and I decided to walk. We bundled up, said good-bye to everyone, and stepped out into the cold afternoon air. A few snowflakes started drifting down from a low pewter gray sky.

It was a long walk home. I was so excited that I had a hard time maintaining a normal pace so that Father Dooley's short legs could keep up with me.

As we walked, Gail and I told Father Dooley about what had happened to Mom's diary and the photograph. Father Dooley listened intently but didn't react, except by knitting his bushy white eyebrows in thought. Then we told him how we had almost disappeared in the church when he first met us, but all that did was make him even more thoughtful. Like he'd said, he had a lot to think about when this was all over.

Thirty minutes later, we found ourselves about to pass Dad's house. We spotted his hot rod and Grandpa's blue De Soto parked out in front. Curiosity got the better of all three of us. We decided that Father Dooley would casually look in on Dad to see what was going on, while Gail and I waited across the street in the park. But as we got closer, old eagle-eyed Gail pointed toward the pond. "Look! There they are! Mom and Dad are skating together! Chris! They're together!"

Yep. There they were, skimming over the ice on skates, holding hands just like they do today. They're a lot older now, of course, but they still skate together like they're young. Like they were meant for each other.

I had to smile. "Looks like it isn't algebra that's on their minds."

We walked over to the edge of the park and watched them from the top of Sledder's Hill.

Father Dooley stuck his chest out a little. "I think we did commendably, don't you? Yes, indeed. It looks like there'll be a wedding around here someday."

"Actually," Gail said, "it'll be on June twentieth, 1961, after they both finish college."

"So don't make any plans for that day, Father," I added, "because you're the one who's going to marry them. And we don't want to change that part of the future, do we?"

Father Dooley chuckled. We all did. We had never felt so good in all our lives.

We looked down once more at the ice-covered pond. Mom and Dad carved large circles on the glassy surface, moving together as one. Suddenly, large snowflakes began to fall all around them. It reminded me of one of those water-filled paperweights that you shake to make snow swirl around a miniature winter scene. Only these were real people.

I nodded to Gail, and she read my thoughts. I put out my hand to Father Dooley. "Father, it's time for us to go."

He looked at both of us and nodded. "Yes, I suppose it is time. I'm sorry to see you leave."

"I don't know how to thank you for everything you've done for us. You—you saved our lives."

Father Dooley took my hand and shook it warmly. "Good-bye, Chris."

Gail put out her hand, too, then changed her mind and threw her arms around the old priest. She gave him a quick hug, then backed away, smiling at him. "Father, you *were* the answer to our prayers. Thank you—and God bless you."

"You're welcome, Gail. Both of you. I'll never forget you." He shook his head. "My two time travelers. It's so hard to believe that any of this has happened."

"And I want to thank you for our parents," Gail added. "They'll never know what you did for them."

"No, I guess they won't," Father said, gazing down at the pond at the two skaters. "But, I'll always wonder if . . ." He studied the boy and girl on the ice for a few seconds. "If your parents wouldn't have met . . ." He shook his head, smiling to himself. The snow fell more heavily, dotting his black overcoat and hat. "Well, I suppose we'll never know, will we?" He turned back to us for one last time, his blue eyes sparkling. "And now off you two go. Back into the future, where you belong. Good-bye. Have a safe journey. God go with you."

The three of us took one last look at one another, then Gail and I turned and walked away. I glanced over my shoulder at the two skaters down below on the pond, then looked straight ahead.

"Let's go home," I said.

"Yes," Gail replied. "Home forever."

CHAPTER TWENTY

We sneaked into the house with pounding hearts and raced upstairs, in a big hurry to take our trip back into the future. We had reached the second floor when Gail suddenly stopped.

"Wait! We forgot the diary." She ran downstairs, then dashed back up with Mom's diary and the old photograph in her hand, her face filled with wonder. "Chris! Look!" She held the picture up to me.

My first reaction was amazement. But, on second thought, what had happened only made sense. It wasn't blank any more, but it wasn't the same picture that we had grown up with, either. It was different now. Our teenage parents were in it, but they weren't standing by the Christmas tree. Instead, they were standing in front of Dad's fireplace—and Father Dooley was standing next to them, winking at the camera!

I had to laugh. "Don't you see?" I explained. "He did that on purpose. He must have gotten Dad to invite him into his house after we left him at the park. Then he probably got Grandpa to take their picture with his Brownie. And he winked just as it was taken, because he knew this picture would take the place of the old one."

"And look at Mom's diary!" Gail flipped through

the pages. "They're not blank any more! They're filled!" She glanced over some of the pages. "The first few pages after December the twenty-third are different, but it looks like the others are the same." She looked up at me in relief. "Chris! That means we changed things only a little. And as time went on, everything straightened out. It didn't get worse! Everything's back to normal in the future!"

I heaved a sigh of relief. "Oh, *brother,* are we ever lucky. We'll read it later. Right now, all I want to do is get out of here before anything else happens. Mom and Dad must be crazy by now, we've been gone so long."

"They probably think we're dead! How are we ever going to face them, Chris? What are we going to say for an excuse?"

"Come on. We'll worry about that later." The truth was that there wasn't anything we *could* tell them. But that problem was going to be a piece of cake compared to what we had gone through.

We climbed up the narrow steps to the attic, then sat on the floor where we had sat two days before. I took the recent picture of our adult parents out of my wallet and held it between us.

"Here goes nothing," my sister said. "Let's give it everything we've got."

And we did. We stared at the picture for long minutes, getting ourselves mentally prepared for the trip back. I tried not to think of what had happened. Or worse, of anything that *could* have happened. I tried not to think of the anguish our parents must be going through because we'd been gone all this time. Or what our story would be when we faced them. I cleared my brain of all this and focused on only one thing—going back home.

Gail was saying all this time, "Concentrate. Stare at the picture. Stare at it. Stare . . . stare . . . stare. . . ." Gail chanted, her voice low and far away. "Concentrate on going into the future . . . concentrate . . . concentrate harder . . . harder . . . harder. . . ."

It took a long time. So long that I was beginning to think it wasn't going to work. Then I started spinning—faster and faster, racing forward into another time, sailing onward into another space.

Spinning . . . spinning . . . spinnning. . . .

I woke up on the attic floor feeling the world and myself coming to a slow stop. I groaned and tried to open my eyes. Somewhere far away I heard the familiar sound of a car pulling into our driveway. Then the sound of the car door slamming shut.

"Gail." I reached over, touching my sister's arm. She was stretched out on the floor, like me. She let out a soft groan. "Hmmm. . . ."

"Gail. Wake up. It's me."

"What?" She moved, then raised her head from the cold wooden floor and blinked. "Are . . . we . . . back?"

We both sat up, shaking the dizziness from our heads. We looked around us.

Everything was just the way it had been before we left.

Gail scrambled to her feet, raising her hands to her face. "Chris! We made it! We're back! And we're alive!"

I staggered up on my unsteady legs, trying to maintain my balance. I looked at the familiar things piled around me, and steadied myself against my grandfather Davenport's old desk. Just the feel of it brought me back to life. "Holy cow!" I shouted. "We *did* make it! We're home!"

Just then, we heard the back door downstairs open and shut. A very familiar woman's voice sang out, "Gail? Chris? I'm home!"

We both shouted to each other, "It's Mom!"

"Hey!" Mom called up the stairs. "I thought you two were going to bring down those Christmas decorations before your father got home with the tree!"

Gail stared at me in stunned disbelief. "It can't be. You mean, we were gone all that time, and we actually haven't been gone at all?"

"Hey, up there!" Mom yelled. "What's going on?"

"I don't know how," I said, "but that's what must have happened. They don't even know we've been gone!"

"Gail?" Mom called up. "Chris? Yoo-hoo!"

I yelled down the attic steps, "We're up here, Mom! We'll be down in a second!"

"Okay," she answered. "But hurry up!" I could hear her footsteps going back into the kitchen.

The next thing I knew Gail threw her arms around me, hugging the breath out of me. "We did it! Chris! We're back at the same time we left! Nothing's changed!" She released me, her face a picture of pure joy. "Let's go down. I want to see Mom."

"Don't let on that anything's happened," I warned her.

"Don't worry, I won't."

We dashed down the two flights of stairs and ran into the kitchen, out of breath.

"Hey," our mother said, turning around. "You two monkeys look like you've been up to something. What gives?"

We just stood there a second, panting, looking at our

normal, middle-aged mother with the gray strands slowly taking over her reddish brown hair, standing in our normal kitchen.

Just then we heard Dad drive up. Not in his noisy red hot rod, but in his station wagon.

It was too much for Gail. She threw her arms around Mom and planted a big kiss right on her cheek.

"Hey," Mom exclaimed in surprise. "What's that for?"

I hugged her next, which really threw her for a loop. "Because we just want you to know how lucky we both feel having you for our mom, that's all."

"W-well," she said, "I feel pretty lucky having you, too."

The three of us turned at the sound of footsteps clumping up the back porch.

"Ho, ho, ho!" Dad called out in his best Santa Claus laugh. "Somebody, ho, get, ho, the door, ho!"

I opened the back door and faced a huge tree coming right at me!

Dad yelled, "Get the ho out of the way!"

I jumped to one side as the adult versions of my father and Dr. Bennett carried a giant, freshly cut Christmas tree through the kitchen into the living room, filling the house with the smell of pine.

"There," Dad said proudly, as he and John Bennett stood the tree up in the middle of the room. "How's *that* for a tree!"

"Oh, darling," Mom said, "why do you *always* have to get such a huge tree?" But she smiled all the same.

"Like having your own forest in your living room, eh, Liz?" Dr. Bennett joked. "Ah, just smell that pine." He took in a deep breath and let it out with a fake coughing fit.

And there they stood: my father, no longer a skinny kid but a middle-aged man slowly gaining weight and losing his hair, and Dr. John Bennett with his black mustache and sideburns already turning a distinguished gray.

Gail couldn't hold herself back any longer. "Oh, Dad!" she shouted, throwing her arms around his neck. "It's so wonderful—" she began, then quickly checked herself. "The tree *is* wonderful! And you're the best father in the world for getting it!" And with that, she planted a big kiss on his cheek.

Dad held on to Gail with one hand and the tree with the other. "What the . . ."

Mom laughed a little uneasily at all this strange behavior. "Don't feel like the Lone Ranger, darling. They attacked me, too, just before you came in."

I explained a little lamely: "That's because Gail and I've decided that we're very lucky to have you both for our parents. And, well, because it's Christmas. And because we're all together."

"And everything's normal," Gail added, beaming at everyone.

"Well," Dr. Bennett said, looking somewhat puzzled by my sister's words, "I'll drink to that."

"Everything's definitely *not* normal," Mom said, hooking her arm through mine. "I still get the feeling you two have been up to something. My mother's intuition tells me so."

"We're just happy, Mom." Gail smiled, letting Dad go.

I gave my sister a quick frown and shook my head once. She understood what I meant and settled down.

Dad glanced around. "Where are the tree decorations? Where are all the lights?"

I spoke up immediately. "We were getting them, Dad, but . . ." All I could do was shrug.

"Well," he said, "go get them. And hurry. Get the tree stand first. This thing's sticking me. I feel like a pincushion."

Gail followed me up the stairs. When we reached the attic, we both spotted the photograph and diary still lying on the floor where we had left them. I picked them up and put them in my grandfather Davenport's old desk. "They'll never know what we went through, will they?"

"No." Gail sighed. Her face looked more relaxed, serious, and even a bit sad. She took a picture of Dad's parents out of the desk drawer and stared at it. "Merry Christmas, Grandma . . . Grandpa," she said to them, then gently put the photograph back in the drawer. "Well, that ends that, I guess."

"I guess so," I replied.

Our father's voice came up the stairs. "Hey! Where's that tree stand?"

I picked up a dusty box of ornaments and handed it to Gail. Then I picked up a box of my own, stuffing it under my arm, and grabbed the tree stand with my other hand.

"Ready?" I asked.

"Ready," was the reply.

And we headed downstairs toward the sound of laughter.

ABOUT THE AUTHOR

Bernal C. Payne, Jr. has been a teacher for more than ten years. A love of fantasy prompted him to write *TRAPPED IN TIME*, his first novel. Currently, he lives in Webster Groves, Missouri with his wife, Marge.